THE SECRET OF THE MARTIAN MESSIAHS

Like a deadly cancer, the Weed was engulfing the Earth, shutting out the sun and rendering the world totally unfit for other life.

First, the suffocating mists came, and then the chaos. Even martial law could not stem the tide of savagery overwhelming all of mankind's civilized efforts.

Man's only hope lay on Mars, where a colony of the world's best scientific minds was working on a project to save the human race. But there wasn't much time . . . for Earth was teetering on the edge of oblivion . . . and Mars would be the next to go.

LAN WRIGHT

has also written:

WHO SPEAKS OF CONQUEST? (D-205)

A MAN CALLED DESTINY (D-311)

EXILE FROM XANADU (M-103)

THE LAST HOPE OF EARTH

LAN WRIGHT

ACE BOOKS, INC.
1120 Avenue of the Americas
New York, N.Y. 10036

I

It seemed to Benbow that the mist had been around him forever. It swirled, grayish white, in evil convolutions that blanketed everything beyond a thirty yard radius of the moving hovercraft.

The roaring downdraft of the great double fans sent it billowing away like storm clouds before a hurricane wind, yet the same suction drew it down upon the hovercraft— an evil, miasmic cloak that carried with it the overpowering, fetid stench of the Weed.

The smell didn't really register on Benbow's nostrils because he had lived with it for too long; it had been a part of his life for more than ten years, and he was as used to it as a slaughterer was used to the death smell of his abattoir. But he missed the sun. Above all he missed the golden glow that was shut out of this dark and gloomy world by the mist that stretched a thousand feet above his head.

Here, on the coast, it was always bad; the mist lifted only occasionally, and for brief periods, when the off shore winds were strong enough to dispel it, and then the hot sun broke through to draw out the moisture from the ground beneath so that the mists returned thicker and more evil than before.

Benbow checked the compass for the hundredth time that morning, and kept the craft a couple of degrees north of northwest. As he left the coastal plain, he kept his speed steady at twenty miles an hour, because he knew that the ground hereabouts was rocky and uneven, and began the climb up towards the highlands. Once out of the mists he could push his speed up to forty or fifty, and providing there were no snags he could reach Machakos by late afternoon.

The thought cheered him immensely. After two months of damp, clinging mist, of hothouse temperatures, of evil, silent nights when every nerve was atwitch and jangling for the ever present dangers of lurking animals and roving gangs, Benbow was more than ready for the simple luxuries of the base at Machakos. There would be a hot bath, soap, the luxury of relaxation for the first time in weeks.

Ahead of him the mist broke momentarily to give a brief two-hundred-yard vision of flat, open country. To the right he could see the ruins of a house, a low, one-storied building without a roof over the blackened walls; the windows were gaping eyes, shattered and empty; the main door was open, hanging drunkenly on broken hinges. In front of it were two untidy heaps spread in attitudes of death that had become all too familiar to Benbow.

Here, under the mist, the scavengers of the African plains couldn't do their appointed task, and the bones of dead men would lie under the gray shroud until time and the elements did what had previously been the work of vultures and hyenas.

Benbow shuddered and put more power to the howling rotors. The fog swirled in again thicker than ever, and buried the broken house and the bodies.

By now the landscape was lifting steadily, the uneven ground was behind him and Benbow made better progress. His spirits rose as the breaks in the mist became more frequent, and when, for a brief instant, a shaft of sunlight brushed aside the surrounding gloom he knew that Machakos was not very far off. He thought about fresh food, of sunlight, of a long cold drink, of men and women to talk to and, perhaps, to laugh with for a while. There was so little laughter in the world today; almost none since the Weed had come to spread itself across the waters of the world.

It was ironic to think that mankind had its back to the wall despite all the great accomplishments over thousands of years—a wall placed there not by atomic bombs or biological warfare, not by alien conquest or human stupidity, but by a simple flower that had grown and spread and adapted almost unnoticed save by a few biologists who had marked its spectacular growth early in the nineteen fifties.

The headwaters of the Nile had seen it first. It had spawned in the wild swamp of the Sud and spread itself across the great African lakes, Victoria, Nyasa and Tanganyika. The great man-made lake behind the Kariba Dam had been clogged by its fantastic growth. In the dark upper reaches of the Amazon, beyond the eyes of civilized man, it had grown and spread, a creeping carpet that had blanketed the waters of that great river and turned it from a river of water to river of weed. The tentacles moved on along other rivers, other channels, seeking, probing, adapting, and growing—always growing—at a rate so fast that even experienced marine biologists, grim faced and pale, were sent back to their laboratories with the desperate knowledge that here was something new and terrifying.

A flower with the innocuous name of Water Hyacinth—*Eichhornia crassipes* of the biologists' records.

Later there had been reports of drifting patches of strange vegetation on the surface of the South Atlantic, patches that grew bigger with each report. The alarm went out across the world, but by then it was too late—the Water Hyacinth had adapted.

No longer was it confined to the fresh water rivers and lakes; it had taken to the high seas, and there, in the vast rolling wastes it grew to islands that were floating hazards to ships of all sizes. They were islands that developed their own special defenses. For the mists that now blanketed large areas of the world had first been seen by the lookouts of lonely merchant ships that plodded their weary routes from continent to continent. In due time the mist banks had become the greatest shipping hazard ever known to sailors. Under them the creeping weed growth fed and thrust forth its tentacles to clutch at the spinning screws of the unwary ship, to trap and to clog the great propellers and drive shafts so that the ship itself was at last imprisoned in a mesh from which there was no escape.

The radio waves of the world became urgent with the frantic echoes of despair from vessels trapped like flies in the giant spider web of the Weed, and for few of them was there hope of rescue. Planes could not fly or land, ships dared not sail too close, and helicopters were too few and too small. The great long-range hovercraft came too late for thousands of marooned sea voyagers, and soon there was no more sea, there were no more ships except those which rusted and fell to pieces in weed grown harbors. The commerce of the world ground slowly towards a suicidal halt.

Benbow's thoughts were shattered at the same moment as the plastic dome of the driving cab was cracked in a score of places. His automatic reaction threw the hovercraft into top acceleration while his frantic eyes sought the surrounding terrain for the source of the bullets which had created the damage. Through swirling mists he caught a glimpse of a ragged group of black men away to the left; three of them crouched on the ground while the fourth stood tall and straight, his legs wide spread to anchor his body against the recoil of the automatic weapon that he held hip high to spray destruction towards the hovercraft.

Benbow swung the steering lever over, seeking the protection of the mist against the greater danger of the band of marauders. The mist became his ally as he heard more bullets clang against the fragile hull, and he tensed his muscles against the sharp expected pain of a hit on his own person. None came. The mist closed in again and the group disappeared from view; the firing ceased as the man with the gun lost sight of his target, and Benbow was safe, heading due north at sixty miles an hour.

A few minutes later he dropped his speed again and resumed his former course, angry that he should have allowed his concentration to lapse so utterly during these last hours of his mission. For eight weeks he had lived on a knife edge of insecurity, every sense alerted for the dangers that existed under the blanket of mist. And now, within two hours of Machakos, he had nearly been caught by one of the small gangs which skulked on the very edge of the mists, ever ready to dodge out into the sunlight and rob, kill, loot and rape, before running back into the protective covering of the fog.

He listened nervously to the howl of the rotors, every nerve alive for the slightest sign that a bullet had done more than superficial body damage. They ran strong and true as they had done for these many weeks past, and after a while he relaxed a little.

The mist thinned slowly as he climbed towards the highlands, following the valley of the Galana River northwest. It was a river recognizable only by the foul concentrations of Weed that clogged its surface, though he knew that below the Weed the current still ran turgidly down to the coast.

Sunlight came more often to blind him with its momentary shafts of brilliance, and Benbow put on his dark glasses against the expected glare. Ten minutes later there was open sky above him with the afternoon sun high and brassy, hazed by mist vapors that still swirled here and there. He felt uneasy as he realized that the atmosphere was still thick and humid, and the humidity didn't clear as he got away from the fog banks. It proved that the mists were becoming more widespread, that even here, on the uplands of Kenya, the effects of the Weed were beginning to make themselves felt.

Benbow slowed the hovercraft to a standstill and studied the configurations of the landscape. Away to the west, half hidden by the hazed atmosphere, the jutting peak of Mount Kilimanjaro reared towards the heavens. Benbow could recall the days, not too far in the past, when there had been snow atop the mighty crest, but not any more. The rising humidity and temperature of the atmosphere had banished snow forever from the continent of Africa—forever, until the Weed was gone.

9

To his right, Benbow knew, the broad stretch of the East African motorway ran its course towards Machakos, and he turned the hovercraft in that direction. In ten minutes the wide, metaled road was beneath him and he poured power into the rotors so that the dust clouds billowed away on all sides.

He was aware that the tension was lifting from him now that the mist lay behind, and there was a feeling of freedom and release such as he hadn't known for a long, long time.

For the first time in weeks he allowed his thoughts to dwell on Machakos and the people he had left there. Machakos had been strong and well organized against the ever encroaching barbarity of the African continent which was returning surely and quickly to the Stone Age. Machakos was strong but Benbow knew that many things could have happened to sap that strength. Suddenly, the tension was back with him again, and he wished for the thousandth time that his radio hadn't packed up so early in the game. With it he would have known—without it . . .

It had taken one week to accomplish the dissolution of the Union of South Africa into chaos and murder, bloodshed and ruin; three days for the black republic of Nigeria to revert to utter savagery; three months for the entire African continent to go back three hundred years.

Only at Machakos, at Lusaka in the Rhodesias, at Gat in the Sahara, and a few other places, was there any form of law and order. But it was a tenuous, watchful existence which had as its certain end the knowledge that civilization was shrinking slowly, and that the Age of Barbarism was returning.

The motorway lifted over a slight rise, and as the hovercraft breasted the top Machakos came into view.

Benbow slowed the craft so that it moved only at a walking pace, and reached for the binoculars that had lain unused in their case since he had left the Camp. From this distance he could make out the barricades that blocked off the main street; he could see the motorway swinging northwest so that it passed a good mile to the west of the town; and, most important of all, he could see men in khaki at

10

the barricade, white men with guns who were watching him as closely as he studied them.

Benbow smiled with relief and relaxed again. He sent the hovercraft scudding over the flat, open land, and as he neared the barricade he saw that a section of it had been moved to one side, allowing just sufficient room for him to enter. He cut the motors and felt the ground solidly beneath him. Above, the sun was yellow and welcoming, and outside he could see the lean, tanned form of Hillary, the marine sergeant, coming forward to greet him.

The door of the cabin was stiff and awkward to move, and he guessed that a flying bullet had probably damaged the metal frame that held it in place. It shifted at last, and Benbow climbed down stiffly, aware that his shirt and shorts were damp and sticky with sweat. Hillary was smiling at him.

"Hello, Doctor." Hillary took his hand in a firm grip. "You had us worried."

Benbow smiled in reply, and was horrified to find that his lips were trembling on the verge of hysteria.

"Yes," he said. "Yes, I expect I did."

II

THE BARRICADE was replaced and the guards resumed their watch. Looking at them, Benbow could detect signs of strain on the brown faces that had not been there two months ago. There were taut lips and nervous smiles, anxious glances away from him towards the open country. There was an overalert watchfulness that had an edge of panic to it.

Only Hillary seemed unchanged, relaxed and cheerful as he always was.

"I'm sorry." Benbow shook himself back to reality as he realized that Hillary was talking to him.

"I asked why we hadn't heard from you."

"Oh! The radio packed up after a week. I couldn't trace the fault."

Hillary nodded. "We hoped that it was something like that."

11

"How are things here?"

"Pretty much the same." Hillary seemed as solid and as dependable as ever, but there was something about him that Benbow couldn't pinpoint. "O'Brien will tell you all the news."

"He knows that I'm back?"

"Yes. I sent a message to him as soon as you were spotted. There's hot bath and cold drink waiting for you first, though. He thought you might want to clean up."

Benbow laughed. O'Brien had been a government official in a district north of Lake Victoria and not far from Kisumu. His knowledge of the people and the country had been major factors in his appointment as Chief Administrator of Camp Machakos. He had supplied the leadership while Hillary and his small group of marines had provided the backbone to his authority. It was typical of O'Brien that he should think of Benbow's comfort first and foremost. He was a man with an addiction to gracious living, one who made a fetish almost of a relaxed and sybaritic life; indeed he was the last man one would have expected to find in the heart of Africa.

Benbow had strong recollections of his alarm and surprise when first he had met O'Brien, and he recalled his later amazement when he had realized just how tough and resilient was the man beneath the façade.

"Has he still got that bottle of brandy?"

Hillary chuckled. "Yes, and it's still unopened."

"Perhaps my return will coax him into breaking it."

"I doubt it."

"So do I." Benbow spoke with genuine regret.

O'Brien's bottle of brandy was a standing joke at Machakos—one of the few jokes that was left to them. According to O'Brien it would be a hundred years old in 1986, and he was going to open it at one minute past midnight on January the first of that year.

He had only five months to wait.

"Everyone else all right?" Benbow tried to sound nonchalant, but he knew that he hadn't succeeded.

"Everyone is fine," replied Hillary noncommittally, "including Miss Garvey."

Benbow daren't look at the sergeant's face, but he felt truly relaxed for the first time.

Hillary took him to one of the bungalows that were used as living quarters for the men of Machakos.

"We haven't had time to clean your own place up," he told Benbow apologetically. "But the water will be hot, and that's the main thing I expect."

"I've forgotten what a hot bath is like," said Benbow. "In fact, I've forgotten what a bath of any sort is like."

"Was it—rough?"

Benbow turned to meet the sergeant's somber gaze. "Yes," he replied bleakly. "Yes, you could say it was rough."

The water was boiling, the soap lathered well, and he could feel his muscles lose their tension like an unwanted skin sloughing away under the influence of the warmth. He lay and soaked while the water cooled around him, and even the dirty, brown scum that floated on the surface couldn't disturb his sense of well-being. Afterwards, there was a hot shower and warm towels from the towel rail, the clean strokes of a fresh blade across his cheeks, and the smoothness of talcum powder to kill the perspiration at least temporarily.

He found a pair of scissors and cut some of the longer hanks from his hair, and after that, combed and smoothed, he dressed and felt half way to being civilized once again.

Until he looked in the mirror.

Benbow had looked in a mirror regularly during the past weeks, but always there had been a scuff of beard, a rime of dirt, a lank lock of hair to confuse his vision of himself. Always his mind had told him that he would be all right once he was back at Machakos and had cleaned and washed and shaved. And now that he had done all these things, it was far from all right.

His face was thin and drawn and pale, the eyes dark-rimmed, deepset, sunk in a face that was haggard and lined, framed by an inexpert haircut that only served to destroy any small illusion of well being. His cheeks and forehead were dotted by red blotches and pimples—the effects of weeks on tinned food with no fresh fruit or vegetables. Benbow stood before the mirror and wondered what Hil-

13

lary must have thought of him as he had climbed down from the hovercraft.

"Don't you like what you see, Peter?"

Benbow froze. She stood behind him, framed in the doorway, seen as a mirror image, cool and tall, just as he had seen her in his dreams these two months past. He didn't turn because the act of turning would have broken the image, would have taken her from him for a second or two that he could not spare.

Slowly, he shook his head. "No, Dru. I don't like what I see."

"I do," she said.

"I'm a walking ghost."

"You're here, that's all that matters."

"No, no, no!" He turned to face her, and they stood looking at each other for a long moment.

At last, Benbow said, "You've no business looking like that, not with the way the world is."

A shadow crossed the girl's face and her red lips pursed to a thin line. "Drusilla Garvey—the whore of the world. Is that what you mean?"

"You know I didn't mean that."

"O'Brien is waiting to see you."

"I know, Hillary told me."

He followed her out of the doorway, his eyes feasting themselves upon her, hungrily aware of the fact that they had been together again for all of two minutes, and he hadn't touched her yet.

Outside the bungalow the heat hit him like a physical blow, and in seconds the cooling influence of the shower had gone. He was sweating again as they walked down the dusty, dirty street. The humidity was higher than it had been the last time he remembered Machakos, and the sun carried an ominous halo that was far from natural and far from encouraging. There were small eddies of wind, like heat blasts from a furnace, that swirled the dust in tiny evil whirlpools.

They walked in silence for a while, the girl looking steadily ahead as if afraid to meet his gaze. Her remoteness was an embarrassment.

14

Awkwardly, he remarked, "You look better than ever, Dru."

"Perhaps I should. They say that motherhood looks good on some women."

Benbow stopped dead in his tracks. Drusilla walked on a couple of paces and then turned to look back at him. She smiled almost shyly. "Don't tell me you're surprised."

"It's just—well—" Benbow gestured wordlessly. "How—how long?"

"Four months—though you wouldn't guess it."

"Four months! But you must have known—"

"Before you went away." She nodded. "Yes, I did. But you had enough worries, Peter, without that. Anyway, you couldn't have done very much."

They walked on down the dusty street, Benbow holding her arm in a tight, instinctive gesture of protection.

"I would have stayed."

"And made an honest woman of me?" She chuckled, and for a moment the old, roguish Drusilla he had known months ago was back with him. "This isn't nineteen sixty, Peter. Gestures don't mean very much in this day and age."

"Sometimes I think gestures are all we have left. The only things that keep us from going under altogether."

"Was it very bad?" She walked closer to him now, and he felt that they were back together again.

"Yes. One day I'll tell you about it."

O'Brien's combined house and office came into view at the end of the street. The weatherboard structure looked frail and badly in need of repair. Paint peeled from the doors and windows, and the mosquito frames had large holes in them. Benbow realized that all he had seen of Machakos Camp told him that the place was running down. When he left on his mission there had been at least some pretense at orderliness and cleanliness. Now, it looked as if nobody cared any more.

"Do you mind?" Drusilla's voice broke in on his thoughts.

"Mind?"

"About me—my condition."

Benbow laughed. "Darling, I'm very happy about it. It gives us something to hang on to. Have you told O'Brien?"

She nodded. "Yes, I've told him."

"He should have sent you home."

"He tried, but when I pointed out that they would hardly be in a position to send another biologist to replace me, he gave in. You see—" She hesitated. "You see, we hadn't heard from you. We didn't know what had happened."

"The radio packed up." Benbow realized at once what she had gone through; there was nothing he could do or say. "Dru, we'll get married soon—as soon as I can fix something."

She smiled up at him. "Another gesture?" She withdrew her arm gently from his grip. "Go and see O'Brien. I'll wait for you."

Benbow went into the house. The front office was a wireless room through which contact was maintained with London and with Denver. London, mist-bound though it was, still held the seat of government for the British Isles, primarily because of strong repressive measures on the part of the armed forces. New York and Washington had gone under in the early days—New York, a victim of mob violence and gang rule and Washington, because the gathering mists drove the government westward to Denver. In Denver too, the United Nations set up an uneasy rule, maintaining an ever weakening hold on the affairs of World Government. The industrial heartland of America and of Russia were the last bastions of civilized culture. China held on to something like law and order, though the age-old barriers were being rebuilt to keep her apart from the rest of the world.

In India, starvation and riot had turned the country into a seething hotbed of tiny states, each warring against the others with a religious ferocity that held all the elements of ultimate and futile suicide. Australia had shrunk back from her mist-embattled coast. Alice Springs was the last important town still under control, and, together with the rocket base at Woomera, held the sub-continent closer to the civilized world than any other part of the southern hemisphere.

All this was part of Benbow's knowledge as he went in through the door and saw the two operators on duty at their sets.

The elder of two men, Carter, a lean, tanned man of

16

forty-five, slid the earphones from his gray head and pointed to the inner door.

"I don't think O'Brien can contain his impatience much longer, Peter, but he won't admit it."

Benbow chuckled. "As always. How are you, Nick?"

A shadow wiped the smile from Carter's face. "You'll know soon enough."

"Is it that bad?"

Carter shrugged. "Get in there before he has a heart attack."

Only a man like O'Brien could manage a brilliantly white starched shirt and an immaculate cravat under such conditions. That was the first thing that struck Benbow as he entered the small, stuffy office. As O'Brien rose to greet him, Benbow could see that the small pencil moustache was as neat as ever, the black hair was smoothed tidily, and the khaki shorts had the same razor edge crease.

"How are you, Peter?" O'Brien sounded for all the world as if he was greeting a guest who had called on him at some obscure and very upper crust London club. His accent was as impeccable as his dress, and the hand that he offered to Benbow gave just the correct amount of pressure to indicate pleasure but not exuberance. O'Brien hadn't changed.

"Well enough, thank you, Michael. And you?" Benbow shook the man's hand gravely.

"Can't complain really. Please, sit down. I've asked Ball and Hillary to join us. Hope you don't mind?"

Benbow sank into the hard chair beside the littered table that served as a desk, and he noted that, as usual, O'Brien's person was far neater than his paper work. Paper work, thought Benbow. God, as if it mattered.

O'Brien cleared his throat awkwardly. "I was—ah—sorry to hear about Drusilla."

"I wasn't. We'll get married as soon as it can be arranged."

"Fine. That's all right then." The elderly uncle act played a little thin at times.

Benbow slammed a fist angrily on the arm of the chair. "For God's sake, Mike, I'm not in the mood for platitudes," he snapped. "Why wait for Hillary and Ball? I can smell

17

that something is wrong and presumably they know all about it. All right, so let me in on the secret."

O'Brien studied him broodingly for a long moment. "We're pulling out tomorrow, Peter." He said the words flatly and coldly. "If you hadn't shown up by then, well—" He shrugged and smiled wryly. "You cut it awfully fine, old man."

III

AND THAT WAS why Drusilla had been so cold and restrained.

Benbow slumped a little in his chair. "You mean—everyone?"

O'Brien nodded. "A jet plane from England lands at Kitui airstrip at ten in the morning. It will be refueled from the stocks at Kitui, and we shall take off as soon as is practicable. In four hours you'll be in England."

The inevitable question rose to Benbow's lips, but before he could ask it there was a tap on the door.

O'Brien said, "Come in."

Hillary entered, big and raw and tanned, followed by Hector Ball, a small, wiry man with a bald head, a moon face and hard gray eyes. Ball was, nominally, the second in command, but it was his skill as a doctor that made him invaluable at Machakos. He crossed straight to Benbow and shook hands.

"Glad to see you back, Peter. You had us all worried."

Benbow smiled. "I gather I only just made it."

"Oh!" The gray eyes widened. "So Michael's told you."

Benbow nodded.

"Has he told you anything else?"

"No. You interrupted."

"Then the worst is yet to come."

Benbow looked curiously at O'Brien, noting the tight lines around his mouth and eyes. O'Brien, he realized, was showing more strain than a man of his caliber would have done except under the most difficult of circumstances.

"What does he mean, Mike?"

O'Brien shrugged. "Simply that we're handing Africa back to barbarity." He leaned forward, resting his elbows on the untidy table. "Lusaka was overrun by a mob over

18

a month ago. As far as we know there were no survivors. Gat was besieged for a week by armed tribesmen before help reached. The French decided to abandon the post and we were the only properly organized base left. We've beaten off two attacks by small gangs of blacks in the past ten days, but things are getting too hot for any useful purpose we can serve. There are reports of a large gathering of Africans at Soy up towards Eldoret, in the Kitale area. Oh, I know! It's a long way off, but we don't know how fast they're moving, and we have a pretty good idea that we are their objective." He sat back in his chair. "I don't think we'd have much chance if a mob in excess of hundred made a really determined effort. The government agreed with my estimate of the position, and decided to get us home before it was too late."

Benbow sat quiet, digesting the news with an ever-increasing depression. He had seen a great deal during these past weeks, but always in the background had been the thought that Lusaka and Gat and Machakos would be there, holding back the darkness that threatened to engulf Africa. But now their light was gone, and by tomorrow the darkness would have won.

"What was it like on the coast, Peter?" The soft voice of Ball called him back to the small, stuffy office.

Benbow looked at the Doctor speculatively. "As bad as your imagination can make it."

"Hillary told me about the radio," put in O'Brien. "You should have turned back at once, Peter."

"I hadn't learned anything we didn't already know—there didn't seem much point. Our main object here is to gain as much knowledge of conditions as we can. So, I decided to go on."

"And have you learned anything that we don't already know, or at least can guess at?" asked Ball.

Benbow leaned forward and rested his elbows on his knees. He shook his head wearily. "No, I suppose not. Mombasa is gone, but we knew that already. So has Dar-es-Salaam."

"Zanzibar?" asked O'Brien.

"Burnt to the ground. All those narrow streets and alleys." Benbow shuddered at the thought of Zanzibar and

19

what it must have been like when the terror hit it. The maze of streets, none of them more than a few feet wide, all of them so crooked and intertwining that in the old days a tourist had to hire one of the small army of guides to make sure that he found his way about. Once a fire broke out, helped and shielded by the mists, all hell would have broken lose. The looters and the robbers and the rapists would have been out in force; they'd have had a field day. By the time Benbow got there, a long time after, nothing but chaos remained. Even a twenty-yard radius of visibility hadn't covered the horror of death and violence, and now, even though he had left the place weeks ago, he could still smell the overpowering scent of cloves as they rotted in the dockside warehouses. Mingling with that musk-like odor was the all-pervading stench of burning and of death.

Almost without realizing that he spoke out loud Benbow told them what they wanted to know. O'Brien sat still and watched him with unblinking fascination; Hillary stared unseeing from the window, and Ball just gazed at the floor between his feet and sucked on an empty pipe.

Benbow told them how he had followed the Galana river southeast along its weed-strewn course until it turned east towards Malindi. Then he had left the river and headed in the same southeasterly direction to Voi. The railroad had guided him through ever-thickening mists towards Mombasa and the coast, and he talked briefly of his stay with an old white farmer on the mainland outside Mombasa. An old man, living on borrowed time and an ever-decreasing store of food, had welcomed Benbow, fed him, chatted with him through the evil mist-choked evenings, and bade him a grave farewell. Benbow had tried to get him to leave his farm and go back to Machakos, but the old man had refused with a dignity that was unanswerable.

"This is my home as long as I live," he had said. "I have around me those things that I treasure, and when I die I want it to be here—whatever the circumstances."

Benbow had left him a few supplies and a box of cartridges for his rifle. It was all he could do.

Mombasa had been a dead town with natives slinking through dark streets, and roving gangs robbing and looting and fighting among themselves. The European and Indian quarters had been wrecked by fire and physical destruction; the shopping center and market were deserted. Benbow had managed to replenish his fuel at the abandoned refinery, but a brief tour of the harbor area of Kilindini revealed only ruined buildings and wrecked ships that had rotted amid the tumbled chaos of the weed-clogged harbor.

Once he was attacked by a shrieking group of blacks armed with knives and clubs, but a blast of fire from his automatic rifle had sent them screaming back into the cover of the mist. He had examined one of the three corpses and found it to be daubed and painted in a manner not seen in Kenya for many decades.

In truth, the age of reason was dying.

He moved southward, following the coastline as well as he was able, past the island of Pemba and the small port of Tanga. The northern tip of the island of Zanzibar had shown on his radar screen, and he had followed the west coast down until he reached the main town and harbor. The stench of cloves came back to him strongly again.

Through ruined streets black shapes had skulked and lurked, threatening him with their presence so that he had not dared to leave the hovercraft out in the open. It was Mombasa all over again.

Southward he moved again across the ocean of the Weed to Dar-es-Salaam, and from that dead and deserted town he had followed the railway lines inland and due west to Morogoro and Kilosa. As he moved into the highlands the mist cleared and a watery sun had illuminated his passage. Once he was fired upon from a barricaded farm near Kangwa, and a group of white men had warned him off with angry shouts and gestures.

He wondered if they had survived.

So, he moved on to Dodoma, still heading west, and at that town he had found only ruined buildings that were blackened by fire; skeletons stretched under the blazing sun. There was evidence of ritual murder and human sacrifice, and on the small airfield outside the town there was the wreckage of two planes. Bullet holes and crumpled heaps of clothing told of the flight of a group of Europeans

21

that had ended in disaster. He had not gone too close for there was nothing that he could do.

By now Benbow had warmed to his story. There was a coherence to it that went far to accentuating the horrors that he had seen; he held his three listeners spellbound as he unraveled the days and the weeks of his lonely journey. It was a cold and terrible tale, made worse by the lack of emotion with which he catalogued the sights and the sounds and the scenes. Over all was one central theme that lay like a shroud—a theme of unrelieved death and destruction.

Benbow himself felt a growing desperation, a depression that was reflected in the bleak face of O'Brien and the tight pursed lips of Hector Ball. Only Hillary, standing like a statue before the window, seemed unmoved—until one noticed his pallor.

From Dodoma, Benbow swung north across Tanganyika through Kandoa and on to Arusha. Here he refueled the hovercraft again before following the branch rail line through Moshi and Taveta to Voi. He was back in Kenya by now, and from outside Voi he could look down towards the coastal plain and see the wide, high banks of mist that hid the lower lands under an evil and miasmic pall. On impulse he had turned once again towards Mombasa, and that decision had nearly brought disaster.

Caught in an unexpectedly thick bank of mist, his radar had failed him momentarily, and the hovercraft had run headlong into a ruined building. The main rotor had been damaged and Benbow had been flung heavily across the cabin and knocked unconscious. When he recovered he had spent four nerve-wracked days dismantling the rotor and carrying out the necessary repairs. At every moment he expected to be attacked, and his revolver and rifle were kept as handy as the tools he used for the task at hand. Twice he had scared off lurking figures by firing in their direction, but the mist was his ally for once, and the repairs had been accomplished with no more than minor difficulties.

The occurrence had shaken his confidence, that much Benbow admitted with a wry smile, and he had headed north along the coast to Malindi before turning inland to follow the Galana river westwards again.

He told of his brief encounter during the morning that had resulted in the damage to hovercraft—and, suddenly, his tale was ended.

"And that's about it." He realized with some embarrassment that he had been talking for a long time, and even the interest written deep on the faces of his listeners didn't tell him that he could have talked on for another hour or more without boring them.

O'Brien relaxed and shook his head grimly. "Pretty much as we expected, Peter."

"The coast is infinitely worse than it is here on the plateau, and the mist is spreading inland."

"You're sure of that?" insisted Ball.

"Yes, Hector. I'm sure."

"It follows the general world pattern," O'Brien said. "The reports we get from London show that the overall humidity is rising and so is the temperature. The cloud banks are getting thicker and the cold air currents off the polar ice caps are warming more rapidly. The increase in temperature sends up the humidity, and the humidity increases the rainfall."

Benbow felt a cold chill down his spine. "How much is it increasing?"

"Last month, July, is usually the driest in this part of the country," O'Brien replied. "We've tried to kid ourselves that the last three years have been abnormal. In fact, the increase had been pretty constant. Under normal conditions the rainfall is around one inch, with an average temperature of 58 degrees fahrenheit."

"It doesn't need a genius to tell me that the temperature is well above that," commented Benbow.

"The rainfall last month was six point two inches," Ball said quietly.

"And the temperature was a mean average eighty three," added O'Brien. "London is under a permanent mist blanket. There has been no break in it for almost five months, Peter. The temperature is up from sixty four to a steady seventy nine, and the rainfall from two inches to nine point eight."

Once, when he was a small boy, Benbow had suffered from a recurrent nightmare wherein he had been smothered by something vast, amorphous and clinging. As he grew older it had passed, and now it remained only as a dark corner in his mind—something to trouble him only on those occasions when he was depressed.

But this nightmare was something permanent, something he had lived with for a very long time, that would be with him until he died. He thought of Drusilla and the child embryo that she carried, and he wondered what horrible optimism the human race bore within it that it could still create life under such conditions.

"What are things like in England?" he asked.

"London is under martial law," said O'Brien. "The seat of government is now at Buxton in the Peak District. Only the highlands are still free of mist—for the moment, that is."

"It's only a matter of time," put in Ball. "Time measured in months, not years."

"And then?"

Ball shrugged wordlessly.

"They need all the expert assistance they can get," said O'Brien. "I think that may be the reason why we're being recalled, as well as the increasing threat to our existence. We can do more as part of the team back there—"

Benbow laughed harshly. "Mike, the world is going to hell in a basket, all nicely trussed up and packaged. Nature is on the rampage. What can we do that they cannot?"

O'Brien shook his head.

"The frontiers of civilization are contracting, Peter," said Ball softly. "We have to contract with them until they're small enough to be defended successfully. Once they are small enough, then we shall defend them. Make no mistake about that."

Yes, thought Benbow wearily, but what do we use? What in God's name do we use?

IV

FROM MACHAKOS to the airstrip at Kitui was a distance of eighty miles across country, and O'Brien allowed three hours for the four hovercraft at his disposal to transport the staff and their essential luggage and records across the intervening country.

By the time Benbow had awakened from a deep sleep that had something of death about it, the time of departure was only just over an hour away. He showered, shaved, ate a hurried and skimpy breakfast, and went down to O'Brien's office. The place was in a turmoil. The four hovercraft—his own included—were being loaded with the records and personal effects of the thirty-eight people who made up the garrison of Machakos.

O'Brien, in a wide brimmed hat, directed the operation as if it was a military exercise. Hillary and his marines worked quickly and efficiently, and Benbow realized that his presence was neither needed nor desired.

There was no sign of Drusilla, or of the other three girls who formed the minority female population of Machakos Camp. Hector Ball wasn't around, and neither were the two wireless operators, Carter and Lewis.

O'Brien grinned and waved to him as Benbow stood uncertainly on the perimeter of operations, and then ignored him, making it quite clear that no further help was needed.

Benbow took himself off and wandered aimlessly in the direction of Ball's house-cum-surgery. He knocked on the door and went in as Ball's voice bellowed an unidentifiable command. The interior was a shambles.

Ball waved a sheaf of papers at him, and then thrust them into a large, leather briefcase that stood open on the littered desk. " 'Morning, Peter. What do you want?"

"I wondered if I might help."

"What about your own packing?"

"It was all taken care of in my absence." Benbow chuckled. "It seems that O'Brien didn't expect me back."

"No reason why he should in the circumstances. Why don't you go and worry Drusilla?"

"I know better than to get mixed up with four women who are in the middle of a last-minute sort out," growled Benbow.

"Well, you can get to hell out of my way," Ball told him cheerfully. "Just remember that we'd given you up, Peter. O'Brien hadn't included you in our departure plans. All you have to do is climb aboard and be delivered at Kitui."

Benbow laughed and turned to the door. "All right, Hector. I'll see you later."

He went out into the heat of the early morning sun; it was a hazy golden orb—evidence of the mist that was creeping slowly up from the coastal plain, from the Weed-covered seas. His shirt, clean on only half an hour before, was sticking to his back, and his face was clammy and moist. To kill time he went back and took another cold shower.

The only alteration to O'Brien's original schedule for their departure was the transfer of certain small items to the hovercraft that Benbow had used on his trip. It relieved the pressure on the three other machines. He agreed laughingly to Benbow's request that Drusilla travel with him, and at ten past nine everything was ready.

The marines had carried out the demolition and destruction of anything that couldn't be taken, and Machakos Camp had taken on the air of a ghost town, a forlorn aspect that was heightened by the quiet voices of the men who made the last preparations.

O'Brien received the final reports from Hillary and from Ball. The entire complement of Machakos—thirty-eight men and women—stood quietly and expectantly; almost, it seemed to Benbow, like a funeral party awaiting the arrival of the bier.

Hillary had a quiet word with O'Brien who nodded and made a note on the sheaf of papers that he carried on a clip board. He turned to the assembled group and looked them over somberly for a long moment, then he nodded slowly.

"All right, everyone, this is it. Let's get aboard."

Benbow helped Drusilla up the few steps and into the cabin of the hovercraft. By the time they were settled comfortably the first of the other—larger—vessels had churned into boisterous life. The dust clouds billowed away around it, and one by one the others joined in until their tumultuous roar echoed and re-echoed up and down the deserted street.

The first, with O'Brien aboard, moved off slowly, and the others followed in line astern with Benbow bringing up the rear. The buildings thinned and fell behind them. They left the road and turned eastward across the open countryside, heading towards Kitui.

Behind them Machakos stood forlorn and deserted, the last outpost of civilization on the African continent was dead now, and barbarism would close in fast upon the heels of the departing hovercraft. The outlaw gangs out on the plains would see and hear their departure, and the scouts would soon spread the news that the garrison was gone. Machakos would be looted and torn apart for anything that had been left, and—if other patterns ran true—it would be fired in anger against the departing white men who had left so little that was of use.

For some reason that he could not understand, Benbow felt an overpowering sorrow and depression. There was little enough in the world today that would dispel fear and apprehension, but even the thought that he was going home brought him no joy. For Benbow, home held more uncertainty than had Machakos.

He turned to look at Drusilla and saw that she was crying.

Even now, after a long and passionate reunion the previous evening, she seemed a long way from him. There was something about her that he could not identify; she seemed remote and cold, cut off from him by a barrier that was more than just a time lag of two months.

In the privacy of her own quarters she had been passionate and hungry for him; she made it the sort of reunion that he had dreamed about—and yet there was something wrong between them.

"What's the matter, Dru?" The question was drawn from him quite involuntarily by his need of her rather than by a desire to pry.

She lifted her head and sniffed like a small child.

"I don't know. I think perhaps it's knowing that the future is so—so blank. At Machakos we had a job to do however futile that job might have been. Now!" She shrugged helplessly. "All I know for sure is that I'm bringing a child into the same uncertainty." She turned and looked squarely into his eyes. "Don't you think I'm right to cry?"

There was no answer to that, and Benbow concentrated on the task of following the hovercraft ahead of him. The roaring motors settled into a steady, all-embracing rhythm.

In half an hour they were across the Weed-bed of the

27

Galana River with its mist vapors rising in the hot sun. Kitui was less than an hour away.

The countryside was flat and deserted, the air heavy and humid, and the sun which rose in the sky was haloed and misty as it had been for so long—so very long. In the distance a herd of antelope bucked and jumped their way across the plain, fleeing from the roar and the dust of the small land fleet. A small group of giraffes vanished around the edge of a large area of scrub trees.

For Benbow, Africa had been only a temporary home. He didn't feel the same pain at leaving it as did Drusilla who had been born in Nairobi, nor of O'Brien whose adopted home Kenya had become. He had been there only a few short years—three to be exact—while civilization had crumbled, while Africa had slid back into the abyss.

He had first gone to Africa as a scientific adviser to the Kenya government on problems raised by the Weed. Then, three short years ago, civilization had been fighting a battle which was already lost. The whole economy of the African continent had been ruined, and for a country like Kenya—only a few years old in independence—a ruined economy had meant total collapse. The prime minister, Mboya, had been assassinated by extremists within two months of Benbow's arrival, and three successors had been unable to form a government. Anarchy set in, and martial law had held the country in a brief but terrible grip. Mombasa had gone first in a holocaust that was shielded by the ever-spreading cloak of the mists, and chaos had moved inland like a forest fire through Mackinnon Road and Voi. Malindi followed; Nairobi had burned for a week, and there had been civil war as the old Mau-Mau raised its anti-white head once more. The Masai and the Kikuyu had vented old scores against each other and against lesser tribes; the war drums, silenced for almost a century, had rolled their message over the mountains and the plains. The death roll had been enormous and the surviving whites fled to England by the planeload.

Several hundred marines had been sent from England to protect what remained—which was little enough—and things had quieted a little. The holding base at Machakos had been born, and there a brief but weakening hold was kept on the surrounding country. There had been large gangs of armed blacks at first, but they had been easily handled by the strong and disciplined force at Machakos. Slowly, the large gangs had broken up into smaller units and there had been a period of comparative peace. Now the gangs were uniting again, and Machakos was no longer safe.

All over Africa the pattern was the same.

It was over now, for good and all, and Benbow was going home again—but to what?

Suddenly he knew what Drusilla meant. Suddenly they were together again, with the hovercraft motors howling around them, making an oasis of the small cabin.

His future was as dead as Machakos Camp and he had as much to cry about as had Drusilla.

The miles fled behind them until at last O'Brien in the lead craft slowed and allowed the other three to come abreast of him. From the large main cabin of his vessel he pointed ahead, and Benbow, following the direction of his finger, saw on the horizon a low group of buildings hazed by the distance.

This, then, was Kitui airfield. This was to be their last contact with Africa.

As they drew near the buildings took on a different aspect. They were broken and untidy, with gaping windows and empty doorways that were cavities in blackened brick and concrete where fire had done its worst. There were no roofs, and Benbow looked in despair across a wilderness of grass that was to be the landing area for a fast, modern jet plane.

The hovercraft settled and their engines quieted. Benbow stepped down to the ground and helped Drusilla after him. He walked across towards O'Brien who was looking out across the field.

"A jet plane will never make it, Mike," he said.

O'Brien wheeled on him, his eyes cold and his expression taut and white under his tan. "It has to make it, Peter," he snapped. "If it doesn't—" He left the threat unfinished and turned to Hillary who had come up to join them.

"Get everything unloaded, Hillary. We don't want any holdup," he said. "It'll be bad enough refueling in a hurry."

"Refueling?" Benbow was as surprised as he sounded.

"But I though a big enough vessel could make a round trip—"

"England doesn't have anything big enough or modern enough," replied O'Brien.

"Are you sure there are stocks of fuel?"

Hillary chuckled. "There was enough to float a battle-ship when I was here last week on patrol. Whoever destroyed the town and the airport buildings missed the tanks over there." He nodded towards the far side. "We've brought a hand pump along to take the place of the hydraulics which aren't working. It shouldn't take too long—if the plane arrives."

"If?" Benbow looked at O'Brien. "You mean there's some doubt?"

O'Brien sighed. "The world today is made up of doubt, Peter. Can you guarantee what will be happening to you this time next week?" He shook his head. "Of course you can't. The plane is due in the next thirty minutes. Carter checked its departure from England before he wrecked the main transmitter. All we know is that it's on the way. In the meantime, there's plenty to unload."

The minutes tiptoed away on leaden feet. Drusilla sat on a packing case and gazed unseeingly into the far distance, shut off in some private world of her own. The sun mounted and the temperature rose. Benbow killed time by helping to rig the manual pump and connect it to the fuel tank, but the job was soon done and he returned to a vacuum of inactivity.

He went back to the hovercraft and, as he reached them, O'Brien climbed down from the cabin of the largest vessel and gave the thumbs up sign.

"Carter has just picked up the plane on the radio, Peter. They are passing the southern tip of Lake Rudolph—should be landing in about fifteen minutes."

It was quite incomprehensible to Benbow that in just over four hours he would be back in England—or what was left of it. He tried to think back over his three years in Africa, but too much had happened. Africa was not his home as it had been Drusilla's. He was leaving only memories, bitter memories that he wanted to forget. She was leaving her entire life, a home that had been burned to the ground, a father and mother murdered in the first massacre when Nairobi had been destroyed. Her mind was scarred by these things as his was scarred by London the last time he had seen it. The difference was that she knew what she was leaving, while he had no idea what awaited him.

On the edge of his hearing there was a minute hum that grew louder, pressing on to his consciousness and drawing his eyes up towards the brassy sky. To the north a silver bullet gleamed, dropping at an angle that had the airfield as its target.

Benbow looked at the long, straggly grass of the field, lush and uncut, gleaming in the hot sun. He wondered if the pilot could make it. The plane dropped down and circled the field. Benbow could visualize the pilot looking down and sizing up the situation, and he realized with rising apprehension that to the pilot the field would look smooth and flat. The plane made a final pass and then swept in low, settling gently and easily in a perfect landing.

The marines detailed as the fueling party had the hose connected in minutes, and O'Brien supervised the loading of the cases and equipment that they had brought with them from Machakos.

"The plane will attract every roving gang within twenty miles radius," he told Benbow. "I want it loaded and away within half an hour."

The civilian passengers followed the gear, and then the marines filed aboard in orderly fashion. The fueling was done and the pump disconnected; the fueling party joined their comrades in the plane, and only Benbow and Ball and O'Brien were left.

"That's the lot, Mike," said Ball.

"Right. You two get aboard." O'Brien waved towards the gaping mouth of the hatch.

"What about you, Mike?" Benbow asked, but he knew the answer even as he asked the question.

And O'Brien gave it calmly and with a smile. "I'm not coming with you, Peter."

"What?" Ball was horrified.

"My home is at Butere," said O'Brien. "As far as I know it's still intact, and there are people there who know me."

"You'll never make it," Benbow told him.

"Oh, I think I will." O'Brien nodded towards the abandoned hovercraft. "I'll take the small one. Fully fueled it should get me there in a little over twelve hours."

"That'll be pushing it hard."

"Remember, I'll be going home, Peter."

"If there's a home for you to go to," said Ball.

"If there isn't then—I don't want to make it." O'Brien looked away across the field and then back at the two men. "Now, get along you two. I want that plane away before there's any trouble, and I want to make a start myself as soon as possible for the same reason. Refueling's done, so there's nothing to keep you here."

Benbow knew that argument was useless. He held out his hand and O'Brien took it in a firm grip.

"There's an airstrip at Butere, Peter," he said. "If things get too bad in England—" he hesitated. "Well, just remember, I'll try and see that it's kept in some sort of order."

Benbow nodded and turned away. He climbed into the body of the aircraft and Ball followed.

Inside a blue-clad R.A.F. technician looked curiously down at O'Brien.

"That's all," Ball told him softly.

"But—" The mechanic gestured towards O'Brien.

"Close it up," snapped Ball.

Benbow went forward and slipped into the empty seat beside Drusilla. She looked at him strangely and turned her head to look back along the gangway.

"Where's Michael?"

"He decided to stay."

She didn't reply for a long moment, and then she said, softly, "I wish I had his courage, Peter."

In a few minutes O'Brien was a small figure unmoving against the vast, expanding vista of the African plains.

V

THEY CAME HOME to an England that was hot and wet, dim with the moist cloud blankets that shrouded everything. They came home to gray land with gray people who had almost forgotten what the sun looked like.

32

In the highlands there were still breaks in the lowering mist barriers, but the valleys and the lowlands had long since surrendered not only to the mist but to disorder, chaos and violence. London was a jungle in which only the strong now survived for martial law had become impossible under the heavy blanket of mist which held visibility down to a few yards. Merseyside and Glasgow, the North East towns, the South Wales industrial area—all were lost to the slipping grasp of civilization.

They came home to a land that languished under the uneasy peace of martial law—where that law was possible—and justice was stark and harsh and violent, with death as the reward for almost any minor misdemeanor.

Despite the heat, Benbow shivered as he stepped from the plane on to the tarmac of the only operative airfield in the British Isles, a hastily constructed, two-mile runway high in the Peak District some six miles from Buxton. He looked at the gray-clad guards, the moist, dank buildings; he saw the ever-ready weapons, the bleak, vigilant eyes—and he shivered. Perhaps, he thought, O'Brien had been right. At least he was out in the sunlight, he was free, he could go where he wished even though death stood close at his shoulder. In Africa the sun had been bright and hot, the mists had not yet shrouded it entirely as they had done here.

Drusilla clutched at his arm and he turned to smile comfortingly, but the effort was a complete and utter failure.

"O'Brien was right, Peter." She confirmed his own thoughts. "Africa was his home. It was mine as well. I should have stayed there."

Benbow said nothing.

They left the airfield in a large, gray-painted bus, and they left behind them Hillary and his marines. There was time only for a brief handshake, and Benbow read in the sergeant's eyes a grim dismay at what he saw around him. Hillary had been a military man all his adult life, and he could read the signs probably better than any of them.

"Be careful, Doctor," was all he said as Benbow shook his hand, and the sincerity in those three words was a potent warning that Benbow took to heart.

The fifteen-minute run into Buxton was made in complete silence. A damp mist hung in the valleys, forming droplets on the windows of the bus. The trees and bushes were wet, the fields were muddy and churned by cattle. Here and there efforts had been made to grow grain crops, but with no sun to ripen them they stood green and lush—and useless.

The road itself was pitted with pot holes that spoke of neglect under stress of more urgent demands, and the bus lurched and jolted its way past three road blocks manned by bored troops in sodden hats and glistening ponchos.

Buxton itself was a gray town. The streets were wet and the buildings—huddling together under the clouds—seemed to seek shelter one with another. There were few people about even though it was only early evening and not yet dark. One or two shops in the main street were still open, but the great majority were shuttered and abandoned, closed up in a manner which suggested complete desertion. Almost everyone to be seen, and they were few enough, wore a uniform of some sort or other, and Benbow had no doubt that uniforms were a fair indication of the general state of things.

That night they slept in a dingy hotel that had been commandeered as a government hostel. Benbow shared a room with Ball and two others, unhappy in the knowledge that Drusilla had been separated from him. His one comfort in this warm, damp, gray land would have been to sleep in the security of her arms. But even that was denied to him.

In the morning an army sergeant escorted them to the Reception Bureau of the Ministry of Home Affairs, and they sat on hard chairs in a dusty alcove and waited in gloomy silence.

Benbow thought for the hundredth time of the open, sunny plains of Africa; he thought of Drusilla's spoken wish as they had left the plane, and he couldn't think badly of her for it. This wet, tawdry land held nothing but misery and despair. It was reflected in every face and in every set of sloping shoulders; it lay in the gray slop that had been their meager breakfast; it lay in the heavy, humorless posters that exhorted everybody to work harder for the common good.

The common good!

Under these conditions it held a sinister connotation. For all that the future might hold the common good was nought but a common grave under the gray, amorphous shroud of the Weed mists.

He had talked briefly with Drusilla at breakfast, but their contact had been cold and emotionless, the conversation stilted and formal as if something had died between them. She had left him after the meal, taken off on some mysterious and uninviting task by a gray-haired, matronly woman, and as she left him Benbow had seen the droop of her shoulders. He guessed the despair in her heart, for he knew that it must be the dreadful despair of a woman who would bear her child in a world that had no future.

An elderly official took Ball away from the alcove after a wait that seemed interminable, and one by one the others followed until Benbow was left alone. Ball returned and grinned wryly.

"Well, it isn't the salt mines. Medical research into diet deficiency."

Benbow nodded. "Making the best use of our talents. From what I've seen you'll have plenty of experimental cases."

"I must admit the breakfast wasn't encouraging. I'll see you later." Ball waved a sheet of paper that he held in his right hand. "They're keen for me to get weaving."

And Benbow had been alone once again.

At least Ball would be happy. At Machakos he had talked of little else but doing research into some of the problems raised by the Weed and all that had resulted from its coming. He'd had a lot of ideas—brilliant, if the facilities were made available. Perhaps, now, he would have the chance to work on some of them.

The same official came for Benbow a few minutes later, and took him along moist, high corridors. Damp was everywhere, moisture clung to the windows, and there was mould in high dirty corners. Benbow knew little of modern architecture or building methods, but he knew all too well that cement and plaster and concrete would not long survive the overpowering heat and humidity.

He was ushered into a large private office, and from a

35

small, littered desk under a high window, a man rose to greet him.

"Doctor Benbow? Good morning." He spoke like a civil servant, neatly and precisely. "My name is Ledger. Please, do sit down."

Benbow lowered himself into a small chair at the side of the desk, and studied the man opposite him. Ledger was small and neat—just as his voice had indicated—a precise man with a thin pinched face and gentle brown eyes that still looked with some humor on the world before them. He was about forty and had the look of a civil servant, an impression that was confirmed as he said, "I am the personal assistant to the Minister, Doctor Benbow, and as such I have the responsibility of knowing what he knows, and of carrying out the decisions which he makes."

"I congratulate you," said Benbow, and he knew that the irony he felt was reflected in his words.

The brown eyes smiled briefly and mildly. Ledger said, "I think your outlook will change in due time, Doctor."

"My outlook will be governed by my environment," Benbow told him. "A great deal has changed since I was last in England."

"More than you know." Ledger rustled a sheaf of papers together. "I spent yesterday examining your record. It is an impressive one."

"Thank you."

"Too impressive for you to have remained buried in Africa."

From beyond the window a rattle of gunfire disturbed the quiet peace of the room, and Benbow stirred in alarm.

"As I said, Doctor, much has changed." Ledger laid the papers on the desk before him.

A single shot rang, muted by distance.

"It is nine o'clock." Ledger didn't even look at the clock on the wall. "That is the execution squad at work."

Behind Benbow a door opened, and Ledger's glance flickered in the direction of the newcomer and then returned to the desk. He ignored the new presence, and, great though the temptation was to do otherwise, Benbow followed his example.

"You are a Doctor of Physics, you hold degrees from

36

Oxford, Paris and Leyden." Ledger read without emotion, cataloguing facts that lay in Benbow's past like islands in the stormy ocean of his life. "You have specialized in plant biology and tropical chemotherapy. Your paper to the Royal Society on semi-synthetic penicillins is regarded as a standard work." The brown eyes lifted from the papers and turned on him again. "Doctor, have you ever done any research on the Weed?"

"Never," Benbow shook his head. "I've never had the facilities."

"Would you wish to?"

Benbow thought for a long moment. At the back of him was an unknown stranger who stood or sat listening to the interview. A stranger who was sufficiently important to be ignored by Ledger. The questions were not merely probes into his wishes and desires, they were designed to provide an insight into his character, to indicate what sort of man he was. The dry statement of facts about his career had been only a preliminary introduction.

"No." He shook his head emphatically. "There must be a thousand scientists working on that problem, and all of them must be far ahead of anything that I might have in mind. There must be other work—other problems to be investigated."

"Such as?"

"The entire pattern of the world is changing because of the Weed. It will be with us for a very long time despite any research that is being done into its possible destruction. There will be a whole new society to be created that will be capable of tackling the problems raised by the Weed—"

"You have been in Africa too long, Doctor." The voice boomed at him from behind his chair as the unseen visitor interrupted his speculation. Feet shuffled on the carpet, and Benbow turned his head to look at the bulk of the old man who moved heavily across the room and slumped into a chair on the far side of the desk.

He was fat and florid, sweat beaded his brow and face, a long, bloodhound face with heavy jowels and a domed bald head that had a fringe of damp gray hair curling around the ears and neck. His shirt was white and rumpled, open at the neck with deep sweat patches showing gray under the armpits.

"The world as we know it is dead, Doctor Benbow." He stated a cold, incontrovertible fact as casually as he might have commented on the weather. "In a few years it will cease to exist, and all your research and your science and your technology will not save it.

"We are fighting a holding campaign which is designed to postpone the ultimate end for as long as possible. All our current resources—feeble though they are—are being put to the task of fending off the inevitable."

Benbow said nothing. He could sense the scorn in the old man's voice, and he knew that he had been tested and found wanting. The old man knew all the answers to the questions, and they were quite different answers to those which Benbow might have formulated.

"We have more information than you, Benbow," said Ledger gently. "Because of that we are able to make a more realistic appraisal of the overall position."

"I have been in Africa too long," said Benbow.

Ledger looked away from him towards the old man and there was a lift to his eyebrows that might have been a question.

The old man lifted his bulky form from the chair and walked across to the large window at the back of Ledger. "Tell him then, Ledger."

"In fifty years," Ledger said mildly, "the world will be a dead planet."

Moisture ran down the window in front of the old man, scoring an uneven rivulet in the mist that filmed the glass. Outside it was raining heavily again, and the downpour swept in gusts across the roofs of the surrounding buildings.

"Is—is this a—a guess?" The question was a useless one, and Benbow knew it. It was a question that he had to ask even though he knew that the statement would never have been made except on the strongest possible authority. He knew that he had asked it only to break the silence that would, otherwise, have become intolerable.

"Would to God it was." The old man left the window and sat down again. "You know Mueller?"

"Heinz Mueller? Yes, I know of him."

"A man to rank with Einstein, or Russell, or Cartier. He made a prediction twelve years ago in which he set out year by year the progress of degeneration as he foresaw it. So far this prophecy has been accurate to a fantastic degree. The science behind his researches is quite beyond me, but the forecasts of that research are all around us now—twelve years after he predicted them. They are all around us and they grow worse as the months go by."

"What does he see?" asked Benbow.

"He sees an increase in solar radiation and in the amount of ultra-violet. He sees a rise in the surface temperature of this planet that will turn the tropics into a primeval jungle, and the temperate zones into a cloud-ridden rain world. He sees the melting of the polar ice caps and the loss of the lowlands to the encroaching oceans. He forecasts ruptures in the surface of the Earth which will lead to an outbreak of volcanic activity the like of which has not been seen since the era when the world was young. There will be a sulphurization of the atmosphere which will kill all oxygen breathing life. Only the giant plants will live, the fungii, the giant mangroves, the Weed itself—these will be our successors. These are the things which will take over from Mankind. This is the future as Mueller foresees it."

The old man stirred restlessly, as if troubled by the story he had told. More gently, he said, "You see, Doctor, your own ideas are dead before they can be given birth."

But Benbow hardly heard the final sentence. He had leaned forward in his chair to rest his head in his hands and to nurse his sickened stomach against the pressure of his forearms. Inside him was a deep, bottomless pit of despair, and in his mind there was only one thought to transcend all others—the child which Drusilla was to bear.

VI

EICHHORNIA CRASSIPES—this, then, was the inscription to be engraved on the tomb of Mankind.

In his youth Benbow could remember a holiday he had once spent on the southern coast. His parents had taken him to Brighton because that was the place where young people could enjoy themselves, and there, along with thousands of others, he had gamboled in the sun and splashed in the cool, clear water. There had been holidays after that, but this was the one that he remembered, this was the one set firmly in his mind, the details fixed and enhanced by the passing of time. The sun had been brilliant, the sea had gleamed and glistened and beckoned to him. The waves had lapped around his feet, sending shivers along the soles of his feet, and all the world held promise for the future.

But the promise had been a myth.

He knew now, without being told, that the south coast was a mist-covered wasteland; that Brighton—seat of his dreams—was a ruined town hiding a few hundred or a few thousand skulking survivors who lived off the loot of the past and off each other. The golden waves were replaced by an obscene entanglement of writhing, leprous vegetation that fouled the ocean and died on the shorelines so that its fetid stench poisoned the air.

He looked across at the old man. "Has Mueller offered no hope at all?"

The bloodhound face studied him coldly and Benbow sensed the brain behind it studying him, weighing him. Was he the man?

He said, slowly, "Your hesitation tells me that he has."

The old man laughed. "I hear that you are emotionally entangled with another member of the Machakos group, Benbow."

"She is carrying my child. We love each other."

"Would you leave her here? Would you go far off and use your talents to help solve our problems? Would you leave her here in a dying world?"

So there it was, out in the open. Benbow felt a cold hand clutching at him. Drusilla would be left alone to bear his child in an unstable country that staggered on from day to day, from crisis to crisis. The birth was five months away. In that time anything could happen.

"She is an expert in her own field. Couldn't she come with me?"

"No," replied Ledger. "There will be no room for passengers even if—" He broke off and glanced at the old man.

"Even if she could make the journey in her condition—and that is impossible." The lined face shed a few more drops of sweat.

So that was it.

He might never see his child, and yet he was offered a chance at preserving the future so that his child might live. There was some corner of the world which was being prepared against the holocaust to come; some area—probably in the high mountains or the deserts—where the scientists and the technicians were gathering to make one last stand, one final desperate effort to wrest the future from the clutching hands of inevitability. And he was being offered the chance—

What chance?

What choice?

He could stay here and watch his wife and child go under in the final chaos which would surely engulf the British Isles, or he could flee.

"Could they join me after—after the child is born?"

"Possibly."

Benbow tried to shrug away his despair. He grinned wryly and said, "You don't really give me any option. My knowledge might tilt the scale. You know that, and I know it. I can't ignore an opportunity of aiding my son's future."

"Your son?" The old man eyed him quizzically.

"The dream of every prospective father—so they tell me." He looked the other straight in the eye and asked abruptly, "Who are you?"

The fat jowels quivered in a paroxysm of mirth. "So —at last you have asked." He lifted a hand to wipe away the perspiration from his right eye. "Forgive an old man his foibles, Benbow. I enjoy watching the reactions of my fellow men, their fight against curiosity, their efforts to avoid asking the obvious question. It is a tribute to my own anonymity—a sop to my soul. . . . My name is Quince."

Benbow sat up straight in sheer surprise.

"You see. My name is known but I am not. And that is a distinction which few of my predecessors in the office of Prime Minister can claim. Such was the power of the press

41

and of radio and television. You know, Doctor, I have always wondered how many people in England would have recognized Pitt or Walpole or Fox if they had walked the streets of their time in anonymity. Compare them with Churchill or Atlee or Baldwin. I am nearer to the Middle Ages than I am to the modern world. I am a man with absolute power—that which the philosophers say corrupts absolutely."

"The corruption came before the power," said Benbow.

"You see, Ledger"—Quince waved a hand at Benbow— "his record is a true one. He has a brain and he uses it. Doctor, you will live through evil times and in strange places. You will see death and injustice because these are the things by which the race will survive. And this, I know, is the complete abnegation of all that man has striven for over thousands of years. This is the plight to which we have come just when it seemed that an age of peace and plenty was in our grasp."

He heaved his body heavily from the chair and waddled towards the door.

"I like you, Benbow. You are a man with a brain, and God knows there are few enough of them. I shall watch over your—your wife." His eyes twinkled. "And I will send her to you if I can."

The door closed behind him.

Benbow relaxed in his chair and wondered. Was this the man he had heard about? Was this the iron man who held the shattered remnants of England together? This fat, genial man with the grandfather air and the face of a cartoon character. John Quince!

"A surprising man."

Benbow realized that Ledger was speaking to him.

"Oh! Yes, indeed. Not what I expected."

"You have heard the stories about him just like everyone has. You've heard of his brutality, his murders, his firing squads." Ledger nodded. "Oh, I know. And all these things are true. That, too, I know. But you haven't heard the other side of it. You haven't heard of the intrigue he has to fight. You know, Doctor, that even today there are men who will do anything to gain power over even such a shrinking land as this. Why? I don't know. I don't think

Quince knows. But he does know that our one chance of survival is to maintain law and order by any and every means for as long as can be managed."

He paused, then he said, "Do you know that we still have steel mills operating? And coal mines. And two chemical plants."

"Under these conditions?" Benbow knew that his amazement showed.

"That is why you had slop for breakfast. Oh, yes, and so did I, and so did Quince. The food that we would like is sent to the workers in the few industries that we control. Every ton of coal and steel, every kilowatt of electricity, every pound of chemicals—these are the things which are important in our future. They are more important than the lives of the petty looters and rapists, the bandits and the murderers."

He shuffled the papers together before him, a reflex gesture that Benbow recognized now as a thought gathering break.

Benbow cleared his throat. "How soon?"

"Before you leave? Not for a week at least. These things are difficult to arrange."

"My wife. Shall I be able to see her?"

"Of course. We're not inhuman, you know, whatever you may have heard. I only wish—" he paused. "Still, no matter. My own wife died in London before we came north."

"I am sorry."

The brown eyes thanked him silently. Ledger said, "One thing that I must impress upon you, and that is the need for absolute secrecy. To the rest of the people here you are leaving Buxton to go to a special research center—a fact that is true in particular if not in detail."

"Quince said that my wife couldn't accompany me because of her pregnancy." Benbow looked quizzically at Ledger. "Is it so hard a journey?"

"There is some danger, if that is what you mean."

"It isn't." Benbow's voice was brittle. "Where am I going, Ledger? America? Australia?"

"Ah, so that is where your thoughts have led you." Ledger smiled at him. "Oh, no, Doctor. We are much more ambitious than that."

43

"Where, then?"

"Ledger's brown eyes were tinged with a kindly, somewhat malicious humor, a humor that was reflected in his voice as he said, softly, "You are going to Mars, Doctor Benbow."

VII

THEY HAD a week together.

It was a week of masochistic torture for Benbow and, he suspected, for Drusilla. It was a bittersweet period during which they grew together with a rapidity that was hastened because of their impending separation. Ledger arranged for them to have a room together, an oasis in which they spent as much time as they could. After the first initial shock Drusilla never mentioned their separation again; she lived a sad, wild dream, and one which Benbow did nothing to destroy because he knew that dreams were all that she had left in this nightmare world.

And in the end he had to tell her where he was going. It was too great a burden whatever Ledger had said. But by the time he told her she was beyond shock, she was incredulous and half unbelieving, but she knew that it was true because Benbow had said so, and she promised that she would keep his secret.

Some of his time was spent in medical examinations and in short, informative briefings with Ledger and several other high government officials. Benbow was one of a group of six chosen to join the Mars project because of their special qualifications. The other five were all technicians of one sort or another, but who they were Benbow did not know, nor was he told.

"Time enough to meet them on the plane," Ledger told him.

"Plane?"

"Of course." Ledger laughed. "You don't imagine that we have rockets here, in Buxton, do you?"

"I hadn't really thought about it."

"Other things on your mind—I know," smiled Ledger. "No, we have two departure points, one in America and

44

one at Woomera. These are only the initial points, though."

"A space station?"

Ledger nodded. "The original Russo-American one put up fifteen years ago, just before the Weed began to spread. It's been enlarged considerably, and we use it as a sort of waystation and observation post. From there, the true spaceships head out for Mars taking men, machinery and raw materials. There are fifty or more of them."

"Fifty spaceships?" Benbow's astonishment almost cracked his voice.

"I told you, we've been preparing for this for a very long time. Remember what I said earlier about every ton of coal and every pound of chemicals? Everything has to be sent from Earth to the space station by rocket before it even has a chance of reaching Mars."

"What is the percentage of failure?"

"From Earth? Around eight per cent. From the space station less than half of one percent, and at the Martian end just over two percent. A rocket is sent up from Woomera or from White Sands roughly once every eighteen hours. A year ago it was one every twelve hours, two years ago it was one every five hours."

Ledger's eyes were somber as he quoted the figures.

"So you see, Benbow, the effort is slowing down. The prognosis is that we can continue for another two or three years, and by that time we shall only be sending one rocket a week. The whole system will grind to halt because of the worsening economic conditions and the growing social inertia—a couple of neat phrases coined to describe the complete breakdown of civilized society."

At other briefings Benbow learned of the mile-long, chain like spaceships that drifted away from the station at slowly mounting acceleration; a thousand ton, weightless mass with a crew of six and often a score of passengers, heading out on a trip thaat would take anything up to eight months according to the distances between Earth and Mars.

He learned of the triple-domed city that had been built just to the north of the southern polar ice cap; he learned that a man could breathe and live in the rarified atmosphere for around fifteen minutes, and after that he gasped and struggled against oxygen fatigue and had to resort to artificial methods of oxygenation—or die.

There were over four thousand men and women on Mars, and every one of them was an expert, a technician, a scientist. Most could double up on more than one function, and all of them had to be young enough and fit enough to make the journey.

Benbow realized what Quince had meant about Drusilla.

On the sixth day Quince sent for him, and Benbow was taken to his small, drab office set high in the converted hotel.

Quince sat at a desk littered with papers, with files, with telephones. A teleprinter stood in one corner, and dull gray filing cabinets lined the walls. The window was wide and airy, and it was shut tight against the damp and the mists and the rain. Beyond it, half hidden by the accumulated dirt, the wet rooftops made a dismal picture.

Quince rose as Benbow entered. "Good morning, Doctor. I must apologize for the untidiness. The work of government is not a tidy matter these days. There is too much to be done and too few people who are capable of doing it. We face the basic essentials and the rest goes hang. Still," he waved a beefy hand towards a chair, "I talk too much. Sit down, sit down."

He crossed to a cupboard and took from it a bottle and two small glasses.

"Whiskey is all I have to offer. A far cry from the sort of hospitality usually associated with heads of state." He poured a generous measure and passed it to Benbow who murmured his thanks. "I asked you here to say good-bye, Doctor."

A cold knot settled in the pit of Benbow's stomach and the whiskey that he sipped did nothing to remove it. This was the moment that had been forcing itself upon his consciousness for almost a week. He had known that it would come, yet he had not truly faced it. He had lost himself in the pleasure of having Drusilla with him; he had tormented himself with the knowledge that they would soon have to part again, and yet he had denied that such a parting would ever really come—and now, it had.

"I leave soon?"

46

Quince nodded. "Tomorrow."

Benbow swallowed the rest of his drink at one gulp, and he choked as it caught in his constricting throat.

"Your wife is a very clever woman, Benbow. I wish she could go with you. She would be welcome."

"Our child is due in five months."

"They will be cared for."

"You will send her to me?"

Quince nodded. "You have my promise. If I can, then I will."

"If I didn't believe," Benbow looked stonily at the old man, "I wouldn't go."

"I think you would." Quince met his gaze across the top of his own glass of whiskey, the bloodhound eyes somber and dark ringed. "Many men have sat where you have sat, and begged me to let their nice, mousy, unclever women go with them. They have said what you have said, but they have gone—in the end, they have gone." He swung his chair around so that his back was to Benbow. "Have you any idea how ruthless I have to be, Doctor? Can you imagine the torment and the nightmares that I suffer? I am not insensitive, but I have to force myself into insensitivity. We cannot send the wife of a technician if she has nothing to offer but the capacity to bear his children. And yet we cannot spare the technician himself, he is too valuable, he has gifts and knowledge that can mean the difference between success and failure. Oh, I know, an unhappy man is no use. That is an old cry from the past—a past which knew nothing of a situation such as this."

"You really believe that?" whispered Benbow.

Quince swung back on him. "Of course I believe it," he snapped. "I have seen it happen too often. An unhappy man will bury himself in that which is next nearest and dearest to his heart—his work. He will work all the harder so that he can forget, because on Mars there is no other way to forget," he paused, "except by dying."

The sudden flash of anger faded from him as if it had never existed. "Every morning you hear the execution squad at work. Each morning I pray for my immortal soul. Benbow, I am a Christian, and every day I do things which deny all the facets of Christianity. I do them because there can be no Christianity without Man, and if we are not ruthless now then Man will be destroyed. If there is a heaven and a hell then my hell is here, now, this day, and I would welcome death to provide an alternative."

He stood up, heaving his great, sweating bulk out of the chair, grunting with the effort as he did so.

"You have my word, Doctor, that when your wife and child can make the journey, they will be sent to you. She will be sent because of what she is, and not because of your desire for her." The cold deliberation of the final sentence was all that Benbow needed.

He got up, set the glass carefully upon the desk, and walked from the office without a backward glance.

VIII

IF QUINCE lived in a private hell then Benbow pitied him, for during the next six months he existed in a similar state—a hell of action and inaction, of doubt and despair wherein hope fluttered but briefly.

He said goodbye to Drusilla on a wet, misty morning, after a night of sleepless passion and regret. They threshed in a web of circumstance that held them fast; they clung to each other in a vain attempt to dispell the future, to forget the present and to deny the past. And when they slept, exhausted by emotion, it was uneasy sleep, disturbed by dreams, that ended in the gray light of a mist-filled dawn.

The same gray bus took him along the same muddy road to the airfield, past the same bored troops in wet hats and sloppy, glistening ponchos. If his arrival from Africa had been dismal, then his departure was unutterably morose. He had been in England only eight days, but even in that short period there seemed to have been a visible deterioration in the overall situation. On the morning air he heard the firing squad keeping its morning appointment with death, but this time there seemed to have been more salvoes than usual. Ledger had said good-bye to him, but Ledger had lost his inbuilt humor. The brown eyes were tired and shadowed, the lips thin with taut lines at the corners of the mouth.

But of Quince there had been no sign.

Benbow had slept in the plane, and he only woke when they were far out over what had been the Atlantic ocean. Now, there were only the mist banks swirling in evil convolutions, stretching contorted, miasmic fingers up into the atmosphere so that even here, where the plane fled high in brilliant sunshine, it seemed to reach and pluck at them. Only once did the mist break to give a brief glimpse of a brownish-green surface too far down to be clearly distinguished, and then it was gone as the Weed drew its coverlet mist close around it.

They had barely twenty-four hours at White Sands, but that was long enough for Benbow and his five companions to look in awe upon a world that bordered on the fantastic. Benbow didn't know what he expected, but whatever it was vanished and was lost beneath the towering majesty of reality. A forest of gantries that stretched for mile upon mile into the distance, raising fingers from the desert to the sky. They were fingers that were gaunt and dark, some only just begun, others half completed, and yet more that were ready to lift themselves and their vital cargoes into the heavens.

For a hundred square miles, set like a pearl on the edge of the desert, the American base sprawled with a vitality that Benbow had not seen for many a long year. There was an everpresent urgency and bustle, a time-consuming haste with a thrill to it that infected even Benbow. This was Mankind as he remembered it from a few years ago; this was Man as he should be, not cowering under the mists, killing to survive, fighting himself as well the elements of nature.

White Sands was all that England was not.

If only Drusilla could be with him.

The night that fell later was made brilliant by the myriad of lights that illumined a canvas which might have been created by a surrealist painter. The clang and rattle of work went on without ceasing as a new shift took over from men who ate and slept, and awoke to work again.

Here, the food was better than it had been in England. Benbow had only four meals but all of them were solid and substantial. The evening dinner ended—amazingly—with

49

ice cream, and as he ate it some of the humor returned to Benbow. In the midst of all this someone, somewhere, had time to make ice cream.

But the humor didn't last long. He lay on a hard mattress and listened to the noise beyond the silent dormitory. He thought of Drusilla and the gray land which he had left those few short hours before; and when he slept, at last, in the early hours, it was on a pillow that was disgustingly damp with the strength of his emotion.

After breakfast the next morning he and the others entered on a routine that had, as its ultimate aim, their dispatch upward into the brilliant sunlit sky. Again there was the overwhelming sense of urgency, the hurry and bustle, the crisp efficiency of a job that had been done a hundred times before and would be done again after they had gone. He had two more medical checks, an x-ray, watched a dozen different forms being processed, and was passed rapidly from one section to another.

And everywhere there was an amazing calm.

For a while Benbow was puzzled by it. The people he saw, the men and women who checked him and examined and tested him, went about their business with a nonchalance and a cheerfulness that was quite disconcerting. There was a strength of purpose that he had seen nowhere else. All that he had seen before he came to White Sands was a dying world with a few small outposts that held on in the face of mounting odds—held on, that is, until those odds became too great. But here, at White Sands, there was no struggle. There was a situation and that situation was being handled. There was a sense of urgency, but there was no sense of panic. There was vigor and vitality where one might have expected only fear and apathy.

The remnants of United Nations might vacillate in Denver; Russia might return to her ancient feudalism; China might build her temporal walls higher than ever. Clearly White Sands and its people cared nothing for external matters; they had a job to do and it would be done.

From places hundreds and thousands of miles away the supply lines channeled into the vast base. Aircraft, hovercraft, rail lines, giant trucks—all the vast impedimenta of modern transport were bent to the task of supply. In the north the steel mills churned forth their products; giant tankers brought in the fuel for the rockets from the widespread chemical plants; the granaries of the mid-west and Canada—not yet troubled by the mists which spread outward from the Great Lakes—poured in the food that was needed both at the base and on Mars. Benbow saw and pondered, and held within him a wonder that was beyond description.

It was a long and tiring day, and at the end of it nemesis greeted him in the shape of a tall, gray-haired army colonel who possessed a tin leg and a black patch over his left eye.

The colonel stood at a bare table on a small dais in a bleak wooden hut. Benbow stood with twenty others, all men, and waited with apprehension tugging at his stomach while the single cold eye of the officer surveyed them from above.

"Gentlemen." The voice rasped at them harshly, though he had no need to draw their attention. "Gentlemen, my name is Kramer. I am the Departure Control Officer." He gestured to a second man who stood slightly behind him. "This is Doctor Honniger. His function will become clear to you shortly."

He leaned forward so that the tips of his fingers rested lightly on the tabletop.

"The speech that I am going to make will be short. I have used it once a day for the past seven months and I know it by heart. I can answer any question from anyone among you, because those questions have all been asked before and they have all been answered before either by myself or my predecessors in this job.

"The rocket which will take you on the first part of your journey is now one hour from completion of its final countdown. When you leave this hut in about ten minutes, you will find a large white transport vehicle waiting for you. As you enter that vehicle Doctor Honniger and two other medical staff will give you an injection and you will be taken to a bunk. You will be asleep within five minutes and you will stay that way for about thirty hours. When you awake you will be aboard a Mars-bound vessel about three hours

51

out from the space station—and you'll have one hell of a headache."

Kramer delivered the speech in a flat monotone, the staccato words of a man performing a chore that had become a distasteful routine. The silence that followed was broken only by the uncertain shuffle of feet as his audience shifted uneasily and gazed bleakly at each other. Benbow felt the cold within him tighten into a knot of discomfort. He realized that he was less than sixty minutes away from that moment when he would suddenly cease to be a part of the planet which had borne him; and that moment would be lost in unconsciousness.

"Any questions?" Kramer's voice demanded rather than asked.

"Yes. Why the drugs, colonel?" The questioner was a lithe American Negro who stood just in front of Benbow. " 'Fraid we might run riot and upset the pilot?"

The mild joke drew no chuckles.

"Yes, we're afraid of just that," snapped Kramer, "but not because of the pilot because there isn't one. These rockets are radar controled. They have to be because there aren't enough men who can be spared to act as bus drivers. There is another reason." He paused and grinned maliciously, building the silence for effect. Then he said, "If anything happens to go wrong you won't know anything about it."

The knot grew colder. Benbow heard himself say, "Is there a chance of anything going wrong?"

"You're all intelligent men. You were told the facts of life before you came here. Of course there's a chance, about eight percent, that you won't make it. The last ship to hit trouble was a supply rocket three days ago. There were no casualties." He eyed them bleakly. "I wish there had been. We can spare people more than we can spare supplies."

Benbow realized with some horror that the officer was driving home a hard and bitter lesson. He was, even at this stage, indoctrinating them to a new concept of thinking—a concept that was a part of the new life that lay ahead of them.

"How do you get the rockets back down again, colonel?" asked one of the technicians who had flown from England with Benbow.

"We don't. They're broken up and shipped to Mars. The spare fuel is used to power the Mars-bound ships. All the metal and the instruments can be used on Mars—that's the way they have been designed and made."

"I don't see any ladies with us," said the Negro.

"We've got trouble without inviting more. They have their own ships. You'll get plenty of time for fraternizing at the other end."

Benbow thought dully of Drusilla and her child. Whatever Quince had said he couldn't imagine them being either welcome or acceptable in the scheme of things here, at White Sands. Suddenly, he wanted to be back in that drab gray town; he wanted to know that Drusilla was near him, that he only had to reach out and find her there.

And he knew that it was too late.

Already he had reached the point of no return; he had reached it the moment the aircraft had left England—no, that wasn't right either! He had reached it at that far distant point in time when he could have joined O'Brien on the open plains of Africa. If he had done that then Drusilla would have stayed as well. No—?

"No more questions?" Kramer's voice broke through his thoughts. "All right, then. File outside and get ready to wake up with a headache."

It was all over in ten minutes.

Benbow was seventh in line—a line of shuffling, silent men who approached the back of the giant white transporter as if they were locked together by an invisible chain. They walked like men approaching execution. Benbow climbed the steps into the transporter, and listened stonily to Honniger's quiet, half-jovial banter. None of it registered. He looked away and out of the vehicle at the dark night made brilliant and noisy by the clamor of work. He looked up at the stars and wondered if he would ever see them again—and then the needle pricked his arm.

He walked forward between the rows of white sheeted bunks and lay down on one allotted to him by Honniger's assistant. Across the narrow gangway the Negro lay humming gently an old spiritual, and as Benbow looked at him the man turned his head and smiled to reveal his brilliant white teeth.

"Guess now I know how Mahomet felt when he was entering Paradise."

Benbow grinned, turned his head away, and slid down a long black slope into a bottomless pit of nothing.

IX

Long, long afterwards Benbow had only a kaleidoscopic memory of the next five months. That period of his existence—he could not think of it as life—held a surrealistic monotony that was never clear. Even while he was experiencing it there was a dreamlike unreality in which only his hungry anguish for Drusilla was true. The highlights, such as they were, stood out in flashes, each unrelated to the others, and none of them in any coherent order.

He remembered waking from his drugged sleep, of being violently sick, and watching, scared out of his bemused wits, as the vomit coalesced into obscene globules that floated in the air before his face. There was the mental adjustment which he had to make, as well as the physical. Mastery of nil gravity conditions went hand in hand with the conquering of acute and unpleasant agoraphobia.

The compulsory periods in the centrifuge were irksome but necessary if they were not to suffer when planetary conditions claimed them once more. The fantasies of unobstructed views of the Sun, Earth, Moon and stars were tempered by the known fragility of the craft in which they traveled, hanging as it did, apparently unmoving, in a hostile and little known environment.

Once the initial fears had been conquered there was only monotony, and behind them the brilliant globe of Earth that beckoned to them even as it grew smaller and fainter.

The arrival was anticlimactic. There was an end to boredom and fear; there was a rebirth of hope and anticipation—and all of this was killed by the same process of drugging that had preceded their departure from Earth.

The twin satellites of Mars made unnecessary the construction of a space station, and the larger one—Phobos—barely four thousand miles from its parent planet, was an ideal base for the ships from Earth. It was a springboard for the final onslaught on Mars, and it was the storage base for the thousands of tons of materials ferried from Earth over many millions of miles of emptiness.

But of all this Benbow and the others knew nothing until later.

There was the same nausea on waking that he had known earlier, the same headache, but the vomiting was, happily, absent. Gravity tugged with half familiar fingers at his muscles, and a reddish glow enveloped the room in which he lay. It was a long, sterile room, furnished with bare beds and small tables. On each bed lay the recumbent form of a new immigrant, and on each table stood a small cup of water and two brown pills. Benbow swallowed the pills and waited for them to kill the raging headache that racked his whole body.

From the other end of the long, barracklike room the tall, loose-limbed form of Larson, the Negro physicist, came to join him.

"How are you, Benbow?"

Benbow shuddered. "Not good—not at all good."

"It'll soon pass. Mine has. Seems like we're the first to come out of it." He sat down beside Benbow and hunched his shoulders. "Hell, even after all this time I'd sell my soul for a cigarette."

Five months! Benbow's headache was lifting. Had it really been all that time?

"I doubt if they allow tobacco imports," he said wryly.

"Well, I'll have to start some research for a substitute from some of the local plant life, that's all. Hey, you're a biologist. Let's get together on this; we'll clean up a fortune if we hit the answer."

Benbow chuckled out loud. "A fortune in what? No money, remember?"

"Yes, that's right." The Negro brooded gloomily, and hummed a few unhappy bars. "Say, there's no calendar either— not like on Earth. Maybe we can work on that."

"I expect it's been done already. They've been here a long time, you know."

Larson nodded. "I guess you're right. Well, for the moment it still feels like February the fourth to me—that is, until they tell me differently."

55

Benbow jerked to his feet, turning away so that Larson wouldn't see his face.

"Hey, Pete, anything wrong?" Larson's voice was anxious.

"No." He gulped down a lump that rose in his throat. "No, nothing. I feel a bit sick, that's all."

Indeed, he did feel sick, but it was a sickness of the soul rather than of the body, and he cursed the fate which had landed him on Mars on the same day that Drusilla was due to bear his child.

Later, when they had all recovered, there was a short briefing by a blond, rugged Swede with a red beard and hard, blue eyes. His name, he told them, was Arne Svenson, and he had been on Mars for seven years.

"There is little that I can tell any of you that you will not learn in a very short time. You are all intelligent men or you would not be here. For that reason we assume from the outset that you will not do anything stupid. There are a number of lectures which you will attend during the first two or three days, and these are designed to indoctrinate you into our society as quickly as possible. After that you will be assigned to tasks which are in keeping with your records and your qualifications."

He grinned and allowed his gaze to encompass them all.

"At this point I suppose I should invite you to ask any questions that you may wish, but it has been our experience that such a thing leads to a discussion that can go on for several hours. So, I do not ask it. You will be assigned to quarters, given clothing and any personal items you may want, but there is one thing you must bear in mind." The smile was gone now. The blue eyes were grim and icy. "Ninety-four per cent of everything we use is shipped here from Earth. One day—and that day may not be too far off—that supply will close and we shall be on our own. Before you do anything, use anything, eat anything, wear anything, think about that."

Dead silence greeted him. A cold chill seemed to spread over his listeners, and for the first time it came home to Benbow exactly how far he was from all the old familiar things of Earth.

Svenson stood quietly for several long moments, clearly aware of the impact of his words, and equally clearly allowing them time to sink in. Then he said, "I believe six of you come from England. Which of you is Doctor Benbow?"

"Here." Benbow raised his arm.

Svenson nodded. "I know of you by repute, Doctor. We are happy to have you with us. Perhaps you and your compatriots will come with me. The Director wishes to meet you all in due course. The British party is to be the first."

They left the sterile room and followed Svenson outside. Beyond the main entrance Benbow stopped, at once appalled and overawed. He heard the murmur of surprise from the others, a combined sound of wonderment that echoed his own emotion. Svenson chuckled sympathetically.

"You'll get used to it," he said. "We all do."

The red light seemed to pervade everything, and this was the first overwhelming impression. Red! Everything was red. Beneath their feet, fine sand, hard packed and unyielding, was red; around them the buildings, all of them single-storied, were red or brown; and high above them the furnace of a cloudless sky spread a dark blue arc from horizon to horizon.

The sky itself was hazed by a transparent roof that lay about a hundred feet above their heads, and this, Benbow knew, was the protective dome that held in the air that was so utterly precious and essential. Under their feet there were no roads or paths, only sand—red sand—hard packed by the feet of many men. Buildings obscured the landscape beyond the protective dome, but Benbow didn't want to see what lay beyond. He knew that it must be desert, cold and implacable, with the sands stretching away endlessly in all directions.

"The air is compressed under the dome by pumping," Svenson told them. "It keeps the protective shield up like a giant balloon, and it maintains the pressure at just the required level. This is one of three domes, each joined to the others by an underground tunnel. The landing area is six miles off, just to be safe, and we have sealed vehicles to bring new immigrants into town."

Into town! The phrase was used casually but it struck a pang in Benbow, and, he guessed, in the others as well.

"We are situated five hundred miles to the north of the

57

southern polar ice cap," went on Svenson, "and we have a pipeline to tap water supplies. The main problem is air as you will appreciate, and we have found that such oxygen as there is comes from the lichenlike plants that are the only living organisms. You're a biologist, Benbow, you will be able to appreciate the problem."

"Increase the lichen to increase the oxygen flow."

"That is one idea," conceded Svenson. "The other is to release oxygen from the rock formations by chemical means."

"It'll take centuries before the atmosphere is entirely breathable," said Benbow.

"We have a great deal of time before us," retorted Svenson. "Come, the Director is waiting for you."

He led them between the low buildings under the thin arch of the dome, and as he looked Benbow's heart sank within him. He didn't really know what he had expected, but whatever his dreams had been the reality fell a long way short of even his most pessimistic expectations. The buildings were rough, functional, half-finished and primitive. There was an air of creaking inefficiency, of impermanence; this was a fingerhold on an environment that Man was not capable of conquering. This was not a new, young, vigorous society raising itself like a phoenix from the ashes of the old. It was a refugee camp created from a hodge podge of salvaged remnants; the flotsam and jetsam of a dying world cast upon an island in a hostile universe, there to eke out a dying existence with all the odds stacked mountainously high.

Benbow saw Svenson looking at him, and he knew that his face was a mirror of his thoughts.

The Swede smiled sympathetically. "I know, Benbow. I have thought it myself many times. But you'll see the other side of it before long. You'll see that this is all we need for the time being. Refinements can come later when we can afford them—when we are established."

"Established?" Benbow laughed coldly. "Will we ever be established?"

"Oh, yes. At first I thought as you do, but now, after all these years I have seen what has been established, what has been accomplished and I know that the pace of advance is accelerating. If we can have three or four more years

58

of supply from Earth then we shall be safe. The people there know it. They have promised us that time, and they will die to see that we get it."

Svenson paused outside the entrance to one of the shabby buildings. It had absolutely nothing to commend it or to mark it as being different from all the others that stood in neat, orderly ranks. It was a little smaller, but it was just as drab. Its one mark of distinction was the number painted in large, black figures on the door.

Svenson led them inside and along a short corridor. He knocked at a door and opened it to lead them into a small, untidy office.

There was a man seated at a small metal table, a gray-haired, old man with a round chubby face and a round button nose on which a pair of metal-rimmed spectacles sat slightly askew. A neat chin beard completed, for Benbow, an all too familiar picture.

Mueller was older than Benbow remembered, and then he realized that it was ten years or more since he had last seen a picture of him.

"Gentlemen, welcome." Mueller rose from his seat and crossed to shake hands with each of them.

As he reached Benbow he beamed and nodded. "I know you, Doctor. You are thinner than I remember from your photos, but then, I suppose we have all lost weight these past years."

Gravely, Benbow shook the old man's hand and replied, "I had no idea that I would find you here on Mars, Professor Mueller."

"You think that perhaps I am too old?" Mueller chuckled. "Well, I thought so too, but I was persuaded otherwise. I cannot ask you all to sit down. There isn't that much room I am afraid, but what I have to say to you will not take long."

He went back to his chair. Benbow noticed that the smile of welcome had gone, the chubby face wore a frown and there were deep lines of worry around the mouth and the eyes. Mueller rested his hands on the top of the table and clasped them in an unconscious attitude of prayer; he kneaded and worked them together as does a man who has a decision that is not easy to make.

"Always," he said, "I make a point of welcoming new-comers, of talking to them, explaining our aims, what we are trying to do." He talked aimlessly and with difficulty—a tired, old man struggling to find the right words to say something that he had not said before to any of the four thousand or more people who had come to Mars before Benbow and his companions.

He broke off and stood up abruptly, turning away from them to look out of the single plain window set directly behind him. Benbow felt his apprehension growing.

"There is no point in beating about the bush," said Mueller harshly. "What I have to say must be said. The manner of the words is not important." He turned back to them and his eyes were at once haunted and pitying. "It is not coincidence that I have asked you here first, gentlemen. You are all from England, and I would sooner tell you officially than have you learn casually from someone else."

The apprehension was a rumbling fear deep inside Benbow, an agony of suspense that tore at him.

"Mueller," his own voice sounded strange to him, "what are you trying to tell us?"

The old man's eyes slid across to meet his gaze. "That England is no more."

The silence that followed was more terrible than the words he spoke. Benbow was stunned, incredulous; there was a semi-hysterical quiver at the corners of his mouth and a tremble to his limbs and muscles as weakness spread through him.

"We heard ten days ago," went on Mueller softly. "The government was overthrown by an armed revolt. Quince is dead and most of his supporters. There is only chaos and confusion. I believe that a military regime held power for a few days but even that has gone now. The latest news that we have tells us that England is finished and there is nothing that can be done to revive her."

Beside Benbow one man let forth a broken sob, but that was all. The rest stood stiff and unmoving, uncomprehending. Drusilla! Her name rang in Benbow's brain as if someone were beating a giant gong whose clamor rose and thundered through his whole stricken being—and faded, leaving nothing but emptiness.

X

PAIN THAT IS beyond bearing does many things. Sometimes
the sufferer dies; sometimes the pain is dulled by the body's
natural reactions.

Benbow did not die.

The aching void within him was still not great enough
to hold all the pain, all the speculation that his tortured
imagination brought into being and counted as fact. Another
man might have turned to drink, but there was no liquor
on Mars; yet another might have taken his own life, Benbow was not one of these.

He existed in a nightmare, walked in a dream, and suffered his private agonies through the understanding and the
help of others who had suffered in the past what he was
experiencing now. He knew that he was not alone in his
pain and loss, but knowing that didn't help one little bit.

Little by little the facts became known over the thin,
whispering waves that bound them to Earth. White Sands
and Woomera sent them such news as they could gain from
the small reconnaisance parties sent in by jet plane. There
was little enough to tell. The opposition to Quince had
grown, and as it grew Quince had to become more ruthless; it was a vicious circle of unrest and repression, and
there was no way of breaking the circle.

Benbow thought of the fat man with the sad eyes and
the sweating, bloodhound face.

"I'll send her to you when I can," Quince had said,
but he was beyond that promise now. He was beyond everything and everybody, shot dead by a firing squad in the
same place where so many others had died.

A military junta had taken over, and a new wave of
terror had begun, but it was the terror of a society that
saw its own dissolution in the mists that swirled ever thicker
through the hills and valleys of central England; and that
rule, too, was swept away soon after, so that now there
was only chaos, with murderous bands roaming a bleak
and desolate land, stalking the mists and the heat and the
humidity, living and dying in violence and terror, strug-

gling in a mesh that was too strong for their puny efforts to break.

But of Drusilla there was nothing.

The days dragged into weeks, and Benbow died a little inside each day, and at last there was nothing left to die. He worked hard, burying himself in those things which he knew best, and that was not difficult because there was so much to be done. He began to realize what Svenson had meant on that first day, and he saw the vigor of the people around him. They worked grimly and with a determination that he had seen matched only during his brief stay at White Sands. Slowly, he became part of that effort; gradually, he was reborn, but the pain was still there, at the back of his mind, even though it was deadened by the laudanum of work and thought. Each day was a problem in survival, each problem had to be solved, and the only reward was a weary body and a tired mind that slept the sleep of sheer exhaustion when the dark Martian night swept down.

Mueller, with shrewd insight, placed Benbow in a research section dealing with Martian botany. A great deal of work had already been done during the years of the occupation, but there remained a great deal more still to do. They knew that there were over two hundred different types of lichen that grew along the lines of the *canali;* they knew, too, that the *canali* followed the lines of the great geologic faults in the Martian land surface, and research had shown that during the slightly warmer summer months a considerable amount of moisture seeped away from the ice caps and filtered along the fault lines. The lichen clung to *canali* and lived on the moisture which they stored and held in a myriad roots and sacs after the manner of Terran cacti. They produced oxygen and they died; they put back something into the poor soil that nurtured future generations. They had diseases which attacked them and which decimated large areas; they fought back with the tenacity that all life shows even under the most hostile conditions. It was the simplest kind of symbiosis.

Benbow did a long stretch in the laboratories examining the work already begun, and it was several weeks before he started to make any headway. So much had been done already that was completely new to him; there was new equipment, new methods and techniques, all of them developed under the stress of urgency. Benbow had to learn them all.

The head biologist, Martha Dresden, was a German. She was a thin, emaciated woman in her mid-thirties with a parchment face and a golliwog mop of hair. She was married—if that was the right word—to a Chinese chemist named Chen Su, and her spare time was spent in raising three sad-eyed children, all of whom were native-born Martians.

Her work was brilliant but erratic. She suffered from spells of acute melancholia which even her placid, unemotional husband could not dispel. Benbow had a feeling that she would have become an alcoholic, if such a thing was possible on Mars.

In her six years on Mars, Martha Dresden's biggest single achievement had been the synthesis of a fertilizer that enriched the thin poor soil so that the lichen grew more rapidly and prospered to a remarkable degree. It had been estimated that the oxygen output of the individual plants in certain test areas had been increased by sixteen percent, and to that extent at least Martha Dresden had produced a miracle.

"We all of us need to produce miracles," she had commented sadly when Benbow complimented her on her work. "The true miracle is that I have survived here for six years and managed to raise a family."

"What was it like when you first came?" Benbow asked.

"Far worse than it is now. There was only one small dome, half a hundred buildings, six hundred people, no children. Did you know my eldest boy was the first child born on Mars?" She laughed harshly. "And my second child was the first to die here. A record of which I am not proud, Peter."

He thought briefly of Drusilla, but long practice enabled him to push the thoughts to the back of his mind.

"I hear that Larson is going to the edge of the ice cap on a field expedition." He changed the subject rather too abruptly, and the woman chuckled drily.

"You want to go with him?"

63

"It's about time, I think. I've done all that I can in the lab for the moment."

"See Mueller. I expect he'll agree. Larson wants to do some on the spot investigation into soil deficiencies, and he thinks he may make some progress if he examines the better irrigated areas close to the ice cap."

And so Benbow found himself outside the protective shelter of the dome for the first time in his six months on Mars.

They headed south in a closed sand tractor specially built for its appointed task. It was, in effect, a traveling laboratory with six sleeping bunks, the whole enclosed in an airtight cabin. It was powered by a small atomic motor that was virtually indestructible; they carried food and supplies for a month—two weeks more than they expected to be away.

They followed the line of one of the *canali* but kept well away from the dull green and brown lichen fields that spread unevenly on either side of the shallow valley. To their right a line of red, eroded hills marked the upper level of the geologic fault, and to the left wide areas of lichen spread away in the clear distance towards another and similar hill crest. The sand was fine and red, but hard packed, and a thin, ethereal wind swirled the surface in tiny eddies.

Aside from Benbow and Larson there was Max Hender, the jack of all trades, tractor driver, mechanic, cook, radio operator. Hender was a big bull of a man with red hair and beard, and he contrasted oddly with Sonderman the Danish physicist who was Larson's colleague in the investigations that the Negro wanted to make. Sonderman was small and thin and introspective.

The fifth member of the party was another American, Hank Calder, a meteorologist who was making the trip to confirm earlier observations made by a previous party some long time before.

The main city had been sited originally some five hundred miles north of the farthest edge of the ice cap, and it was estimated that two days would be enough for the tractor to make the trip; that, together with the return journey, would allow them ten days for such observaions as they wished to make.

Five miles away from the domed city they crested the hills and moved south over a wide, flat plain. The *canali* swept away to the westward and beyond their sight. Here, on the other side of the hill range, Benbow had his first sight of one of the four small oxygen plants that had been built to add their minute output to that of the native lichen. As on Earth the main construction of the Martian soil and rock formation was oxygen and silicon, and the chemical release of the oxygen was a necessary adjunct to the survival of the domes.

From the four plants the oxygen was piped to the cities, the surplus being discharged into the atmosphere where, after a thousand years, it might make some appreciable difference.

Benbow felt a pang as he looked at the plant. He saw it there, squatting at the base of the hills, and he knew what had gone into it and realized how small was the result of such an effort. Did any of it really matter? All around them the red sands stretched endlessly away, a vast, forbidding ocean in which the tractor was the only moving thing.

"Anything wrong, Peter?" Larson, sitting next to him, had caught the gaunt hopelessness which Benbow knew must be written on his face.

He shrugged. "No more than usual."

"Martha told me you'd done a good job in the lab."

"Trying to cheer me up? Don't bother."

"Look, Peter, I thought it was all behind you. After all—"

"It's been six months," Benbow interrupted. "I know. It's as far behind me as it will ever be. Anyway, it's not that."

"What then?"

For a long time Benbow had held within him a core of depression, a doubt, a seed that had grown like a cancer, nourished by an inquiring mind and a complete lack of emotion He knew that he did not possess the driving urge, the grim determination, that inspired almost all the others gathered beneath the flimsy domes. He worked and slogged because that was his escape, a soporific that sent him wearily to bed; a drug that killed his thoughts and dreams.

65

There had been a clue here, a doubt there. Martha Dresden's work had been brilliant, but there were questions about the effectiveness of her work. Benbow had asked himself often if what she had done was enough—and, of course, the answer was no. The answer was always no. Everything that had been done on Mars was a triumph of planning and work and thought; but in everything that he saw Benbow asked himself the same question, was it enough? And always he got the same answer.

Of late his doubts had crystalized, and his reasons for wanting to make a field trip had been two-fold. The first set were the ones that he had given to Mueller—that he wanted to follow up his work in the laboratory by making on-the-spot researches into the lichen and their function. The second and true reason—the one which he kept locked within himself—was the gnawing doubt that all was not as it should be—a nebulous something that he could not exactly define.

"What then?" insisted Larson.

Benbow shrugged again. "A feeling, that's all." He looked at the red desert, and a chill wind seemed to blow through him as he realized for the first time just what that feeling was.

"Larson," he said softly, "this isn't going to work."

The Negro shifted uncomfortably. "Hey, Pete, you bugged or something?"

"No, I'm just seeing Mars for the first time, and I've realized that this whole damned project just isn't going to work—and what's more, I think Mueller knows it too."

"Are you crazy?"

"No, I'm saner than any of you. I haven't got the same pie-in-the-sky, starry-eyed enthusiasm of the rest of you—"

"Four thousand people can't be wrong."

"Oh, I think some of them know—the hierarchy like Mueller and Svenson and Chen Su. I shouldn't be surprised if Martha knows as well—in fact, she's the only one who shows it. The rest of them are acting a part, Larson, and I've only just begun to realize it."

XI

IF BENBOW expected Larson to take notice of him then he was disappointed. The gangling Negro ignored his outburst and tried to laugh the matter away.

They headed south into the area known as Hellespont, and here the land was dead flat, stretching monotonously away on all sides. It was a cold, red land beside which the deserts of Earth seemed warm and welcoming. Directly overhead where the deep blue of the sky was almost black, the faint glimmer of the brighter stars could be seen, even though it was almost midday. The low hills were lost behind them now, and, with the ground flat and even, Hender poured power into the tractor's motors until they were making a good forty miles an hour.

They stopped in mid-afternoon for a meal, and the temperature was high enough for them to step outside without too much protective clothing.

"By dusk," Sonderman told Benbow, "it'll be down to minus one hundred and still falling. So tonight we sleep inside."

Benbow had known that the Martian nights were cold, but he had been cosseted against the knowledge by the artificial temperature beneath the domes. The thin Dane's words brought home to him just how hostile a world Mars could be.

He tried the experiment of breathing the thin air without his face mask, and he found that he could breathe comfortably and without effort provided he didn't make any physical effort. Two or three steps started him gasping, his heart pounding within him, and he knew the truth that a man could indeed survive for only fifteen minutes without artificial aid.

By early afternoon the next day they were within sight of the white expanse of the southern ice cap. It was mid-autumn and the ice cap had shrunk by several score miles from its furthermost limits. They halted on the edge of wide areas of vegetation, the largest and lushest that they had seen. In some places the dark green plants grew to a height of several inches and the leaves were thick and heavy.

By no stretch of imagination could these be called lichen, but it was the nearest form of life on Earth that could be reasonably compared to that on Mars. And so, lichen it had become.

A few hundred yards away the sand was lost beneath a thin, white covering that looked like a heavy frost. Darker areas of sand stood out here and there like blotches on a pure white skin, and Benbow noticed that the soil was darker and richer than any he had yet seen.

"We've got an hour or two before sunset," Larson said. "We can get the small dome rigged and store some of the gear, ready to start work tomorrow."

"Is this as far as we're going?" asked Benbow.

Sonderman chuckled. "This is the edge of the ice cap, Peter. This is our destination."

Benbow looked at the landscape in amazement. "This? But there isn't any ice!"

"What did you expect?" asked the Dane. "Icebergs, like in Greenland?"

"No, but—"

"Peter, get used to the fact that Mars is a dry world," put in Larson. "Closer to the pole there are twelve or fourteen inches of snow, some of it hard packed. But that's all. Out here at this time of the year there's only a sprinkling—no more than three inches in the thickest part."

So Benbow stored away another fact.

The portable dome which they had brought with them was inflated over a metal frame to a height of seven feet and a diameter of twenty feet. It had an airlock and a pump for maintaining pressure, and inside it they could work in comparative comfort. The tractor remained their living quarters.

They started work the next day, and Benbow's first task was to gather samples of the various lichens and plants. He had seen from the lab records and reports back at the main city that the areas of lushest vegetation were those close to the poles, and it was recognized that a great deal of the vegetation in these areas was of a highly developed nature. Experiments had shown that the plant life had to withstand temperatures which varied from minus one forty fahrenheit to more than eighty degrees plus. Flora with that resilience would clearly respond to a richer soil and a greater moisture.

The problem was to create these conditions over sufficiently large areas to improve the plant life and to bring about a far greater output of natural oxygen.

Benbow had thought a great deal about the problem, but he said nothing to Larson, and the party went about its work with the same dogged determination that he had seen at the base. Sonderman worked with Larson on his soil investigations, while Calder was exclusively employed with his meteorological equipment. Hender cooked and cleaned, kept the tractor in good shape, and helped out generally whenever he was wanted.

The days slid by and Benbow learned a good deal. There was, as he already knew, a good deal more to Martian flora than just simple lichen. True, most of the plant life was lichenlike in construction, but the more advanced vegetation was completely different from any species that he had known on Earth.

On the morning of the eighth day of their camp he decided to head deep into one of the more abundant areas of growth that lay close by, in an effort to determine just how the plants in the central areas differed from those towards the edges. Larson had already made one trip, and his researches had confirmed that the soil was considerably better than any they had come across within the immediate vicinity of the main base.

"It's still poor stuff compared with Earth," he told Benbow. "But it's better than most. More minerals in it to start with, and you know how important that is."

"I'd like to take a look myself," said Benbow.

"Martha was up here herself about a year ago, but I don't think she got as far as we have," put in Sonderman. "The area Larson and I covered is a good three miles off. You'd better get Hender to go with you."

"No need. I'll be in sight of the tractor for most of the time," Benbow replied. "If I get away early I should have three or four hours at the site before I need to turn back."

He got away as soon as breakfast was over, and he carried a shoulder pack with portable equipment and a short range radio. Larson's earlier trip had left a pathway that was still clear, and Benbow followed it with no trouble at all. It took him almost an hour to reach the spot where disturbed soil and trampled vegetation showed that Larson had been at work, and his first sight of the soil told him that it was indeed far richer and darker than any he had yet seen. The plants themselves were larger and more luxuriant, although even here they were poor specimens compared with the average Terran desert flower. They rose on thick stalks to a height of some eight or ten inches, and they clustered in groups, each species keeping separate from all the others.

Benbow worked steadily for an hour or more gathering specimens and carrying out such on-the-spot tests as he could manage with his limited equipment. In his protective suit he was soon sweating heavily, once the small disc of the sun had risen high in sky. He guessed that the temperature was now well over the forties, and from where he stood he could see a thin, ethereal mist—almost unoticeable unless one was looking for it—rising from the snow fields. The humidity of the air was less than one percent, but the limits of the ice cap ebbed and flowed like a gentle sea tide between dawn and dusk, and dusk and dawn.

It was almost midday when Hender came on the radio, calling him by name.

"Benbow, this is Hender at base. Are you receiving me?"

"Hello, Max. Benbow. What is it?"

"You'd better head back," Hender told him. "Calder's picked up a disturbance on his gadgets that's building up and heading this way fast."

Benbow stood up from his task and stretched his aching back.

"Is Hank there?" he asked.

"Sure. I'll put him on."

Hender's voice faded, and seconds later the thick accent of Calder rang tinnily in Benbow's ears.

"Better head back fast, Pete. There's a dilly of a storm building up—"

"A storm?" Benbow couldn't keep the incredulity out of his voice.

"Sand storm. We get them once in a while, especially at this time of the year. You'd better head back—and fast."

"Right. I'm on my way."

Benbow began to clear up his scattered belongings. He packed the specimens carefully in special containers, took down his equipment and packed it away in his shoulder carrier. As he stood up he was facing northwards, and the sky sloped down to the horizon, a vast arc of deep blue that faded into red at the base of the arc. And there, low down on the horizon, but rising even as he looked at it, was a swirling red cloud. It moved slowly, lazily like a genie rising from a mythical bottle, boiling up into fantastic shapes that circled and spread and then were dissipated as a smoke cloud is destroyed. As he watched it with a mixture of awe and horror the sound of it reached his ears even through the protective helmet. A high, thin whining that rose and fell, keening with a mournfulness that struck fear inside him; the first movement of air around him told Benbow that he had stayed too long.

He shouldered the pack and headed back along the path that led to the tractor. The high arc of the sky was shadowed now, and tiny eddies of sand blew around his feet. The keening grew louder and the air moved more violently bringing with it a panic that lent speed to his feet. The tractor was in sight now, and all around him the sand between the vegetation sprang into a horrible life of its own, moving with an evil volition that seemed to enmesh his hurrying feet.

Beside the tractor he could see small figures working to anchor the dome, and as he looked, a thick plant stalk clutched at his feet and sent him sprawling. The wind plucked at him as he struggled up and hurried on; his helmet rang and rustled as the sand beat against it, and then—suddenly—the tractor was gone.

Benbow halted dead in his tracks.

Visibility had dropped to less than five yards, and around him the weird screeching of the storm battered at his senses with unimaginable violence. He dared not go on. The tractor had been perhaps half a mile straight ahead of him, but the swirling sands had blotted out the path that he had been following, and before him was only a wall of

71

red, impenetrable sand that beat against him like a living entity.

To his left, just on the edge of his vision, Benbow could see one of the thicker patches of vegetation. The stalks were bending before the wind, but they were not breaking, and they formed a barrier some eight inches high against which the screeching storm battered and tore. Benbow did the only thing possible, but there was panic in his heart as he did it. He threw himself flat on his stomach and burrowed his head in between the plants, seeking the poor shelter that they offered.

The wind tore at his protective clothing, and the sand rasped and rattled like a million tiny animals scratching and seeking entrance. Around him he could feel the sand piling up, and he remembered one of the lectures that he had attended during his first days on Mars, a lecture that explained how the vast areas of vegetation were sometimes completely obliterated by a really vicious sand storm. It ripped at the plants and tore at the roots, and when the storm had passed there was only desert where earlier the tough, resilient vegetation had clung with such tenacity.

The panic grew stronger. He wanted to get up and run and find the tractor, but he didn't know in which direction it lay. The sand was piling up around him, and it seemed momentarily more difficult to breathe as he lay in a dark, roaring world that was like a tomb in the middle of hell.

He didn't recall when consciousness left him, but his mind sought the darkness as a protection against the storm, and it faded from his ken.

XII

BENBOW CAME to with the choking agony of claustrophobia tugging at his throat. It was dark, pitch dark and he seemed to be held by an unyielding but amorphous blanket that pressed on him from all sides. He moved his arms with difficulty and there was a dry rustling around his head as the sand moved and shifted.

But most of all there was silence.

After that initial movement his limbs were held fast, and

72

the only noise was the dry rasping of his breath inside the helmet. Strangely, he didn't feel panic as he had done before he lost consciousness; he knew that he was covered by a shroud of sand which had drifted and spun around him as the storm had followed its chaotic course. It might only be inches deep above him; it might be piled upon him so that all possibility of extricating himself was gone.

Then he realized that there appeared to be no weight pressing down on him, a gentle pressure to be sure, but that was all. He heaved himself up, struggling to rise from his prone position. There was an instant of resistance and then something gave and he got to his knees with his rump higher than his head. The dry, ethereal rasping rang in his ears, and over that sound he could hear voices that were dull and hazed by the sand and by his helmet. He struggled again to lift his head, and as he felt it move there were arms at his shoulders and hands that pulled him upwards from the living grave of red sand.

As the darkness lifted he realized that all he could see was the inside of his helmet a bare two inches in front of his nose.

"You all right, Peter?" Larson's voice boomed at him, high with a mixture of relief and anxiety.

"Yes, I think so. What's wrong with this helmet? I can't see a damned thing."

"The sand has got at it," Larson told him. "You'll have to get another when we get back to base. The damned stuff has rubbed it opaque." He put a hand under Benbow's elbow. "Come on, we'll guide you back."

The trip back to the tractor was eerie; Hender took his other arm, and—stumbling often—he was led like a blind man the half mile or so back to base.

Once inside the vehicle he stripped off the helmet and slumped on the bunk with a sigh of relief.

"You had us worried." Sonderman handed him a hot drink. "We saw you disappear in the storm but there wasn't a thing that we could do."

"How long was I out there?"

"Two hours," Hender told him.

"It might have been forever if Hank hadn't given me a bit of warning." Benbow sipped at the scalding coffee. "Did you manage to rescue the specimens and the equipment?"

"All here," grinned Sonderman.

Benbow sighed. "At least I won't have to go back without them. Has the storm gone for good?"

"Yeah, headed clean over the pole," Calder said. "I don't think we'll get another for a while."

"Even so, I think we'll head back to base." Larson was looking out of the tractor across the sandy waste. "There's no point in staying here."

"But we've got two more days," objected Benbow. "You're not going back because of me, are you?"

Larson chuckled. "You value yourself too highly, Peter. No, it's simply that there isn't any point in staying now." He gestured out of the port. "We'd have to go the best part of a hundred miles to pick up where we were before the storm hit us."

Benbow stood up shakily and followed the direction of his gaze. All around stretched the red blanket of desert with which he had become so familiar. The snow line was gone, buried under the might of the storm; the wide acres of vegetation had disappeared, and where green leaves and thick stalks had grown there was now only the eternal sand of Mars.

The coffee had done nothing to warm him, and he still felt cold inside; it was a coldness that was more terrifying than anything he had ever known in his life before. He wanted desperately to be back on Earth, with the Weed, the mists, the chaos, the heat—and with Drusilla to hold on to. The tractor expedition had done nothing save increase his conviction that the whole crazy setup on Mars was doomed to failure before it had even begun. Ten years was an instant in eternity, and Mars had eternity written deep in her shifting sands. He shuddered and wondered what would be left here in another ten years; at the back of his mind was an overwhelming conviction that the desert would be washing over his bones and claiming that which had so recently escaped the clutching fingers of sand.

They left at dawn the next day, and Hender drove the tractor hard so that by noon of the following day they were in sight of the low hill range that was the main land mark for the base city.

During their absence another group of technicians had arrived from Earth, and Benbow—after a hurried meal—sought them out to make his usual desperate inquiries. There were no men from England in the group which was the first to leave White Sands after the collapse of the British government. All any of them knew was that Quince's regime had failed and that the military rule that followed him had lasted only a few days. True, there had been a few people who had managed to get away in the sole jet plane to make the Atlantic crossing, and there had been rumors of two hovercraft that had been ready and waiting to get clear—but that was all.

Tired and dispirited, Benbow went to his dormitory and slept until late evening.

When he awoke he lay on his hard cot for a long time and thought and wondered. There were facts to be marshaled, ideas to be correlated, and when at last he was clear in his own mind, he got up, dressed and went in search of Heinz Mueller.

The old man lived in the small hut which was also his office, control center, record bureau—and home. There was hardly an hour, day or night, when he could not be found there, working. It was only half the size of any of the other buildings that nestled under the Martian domes, and it was the one status symbol that was possessed by anyone on Mars.

But then, Mueller was something special.

A light burned in the office when Benbow got there, and he knocked before going in. Mueller was there, eternally behind his small, littered desk, and Benbow wondered if, in fact, the old man ever left that worn and battered chair. Svenson was there as well, leaning against a filing cabinet, his feet crossed and his arms akimbo.

"Am I disturbing anything?" Benbow asked.

"No, no. Come in, Peter." Mueller waved him to the only other chair in the small room. "Svenson has been discussing the future of the base, with expansion and so on. We shall have to raise two more domes before long. You see," he smiled, "we are growing.

"Oh, yes. I heard about your unfortunate experience. Glad you're all right."

75

Benbow sat quiet, uncertain what to say, how to begin. He had not counted on Svenson being present.

"Well?" urged Mueller quietly.

"I really wanted to talk to you alone, Mueller. No offence to you," he added hurriedly to the Swede.

The rheumy old eyes twinkled at him from behind the ancient spectacles that were set, as always, half way down the red button of the old man's nose. "Arne knows what I know, Peter. It is the only way. I am an old man."

Outside the single window the night was dark and silent. The base was at its quietest at this time, and that quietude seemed amplified a hundred times as Benbow said, softly, "All right. I have this to say, Mueller. This whole scheme is impossible. In ten years time there won't be anything here but desert—and I believe you know it as well as I do."

And still the old eyes smiled at him.

"What makes you so pessimistic?" asked Mueller mildly.

"You see," snapped Benbow, "you aren't even surprised or shocked at such an idea."

"Other people have come here and expressed just the same doubts and fears," said Svenson.

"And you have managed to convince them otherwise. All right, convince me," rasped Benbow. "Mueller, you're too big a man to go along with a fraud like this unless there is something much bigger than anyone can guess at. Go on, tell me I'm wrong. Tell me that you know something that I don't."

"First, you tell me what you think, Peter." Mueller relaxed in his chair and folded his hands across his ample stomach. "Please, tell me everything. It is important that I know."

"All right." Benbow leaned forward and rested his elbows on his knees, folding his hands together before his face, and allowing his thoughts to run into the channels which he had planned. "First, it's quite clear to me that this base can never be self-supporting with a population of around five thousand. Oh, I know that the hydroponics are being increased, but they rely on water, and there is too little water available. I know, I've just seen the Martian ice caps. Second, once the bases at White Sands and Woomera go under everything stops. No more food, no more chemicals, no more raw materials, no more anything."

"There are metals here, on Mars," said Svenson mildly.

"You can't eat metal," Benbow said savagely. "From somewhere you have to produce four thousand tons of food in a Terran year simply to maintain the people at a minimum level. All right, so you've got stuff stockpiled all over the place, but you can't replace more than one percent of it from your hydroponic gardens or your yeast factory. You can't grow corn or wheat or maize, you can't raise cattle or sheep or pigs or chickens. You'll have to maintain a strict control on births, you'll have to ration water."

Wearily, Benbow shook his head. The fire had gone from him as he spoke because now his ideas were being free expression, they were out in the open for the first time, and at last he knew how futile was this puny attempt at salvation.

"It just will not work, Mueller. You have got to plan for a thousand years ahead, not for a decade, not even for a century. If you can convince me that you are planning for the next millenium, then you'll have to have an ace up your sleeve somewhere, and right now I can't see one existing."

Mueller smiled and nodded and said nothing.

Benbow said, "I have studied the Martian flora long enough and hard enough to know that we must seek our salvation somewhere else. True, they store water, but in themselves they possess nothing save perhaps fiber that could be turned into cloth. They have an entirely different biologic structure to anything we know on Earth, and for that reason alone I doubt if we can ever live in any form of symbiosis with them. Why, even to fertilize them Martha had to come up with something utterly new in concept and execution.

"There is something else." Benbow paused and looked at each of them. "Something which I cannot believe you have overlooked entirely."

"And what is that?" inquired Mueller.

"Any organization which has to live as we do, under a dome to protect us, is doomed from the start. The oxygen content of the air will have to be increased by a fantastic

77

amount before we can stay outside for any length of time. And even then—once we can go outside—we have to contend with extremes of heat and cold between day and night To do that we need the equipment of an arctic explorer on Earth."

Benbow sat up straight in the chair and looked bleakly at Mueller.

"Have I talked enough? Or do you want some more?"

"You have missed one or two points, Peter—"

"Such as?"

Mueller spread his hands wide. "The human element involved. You have not asked what will happen once the supply lines from Earth dry up. When everyone knows that White Sands is gone the way of Buxton. When Woomera has been swallowed by the desert and the mists."

"All right," snapped Benbow. "I'll write you a thesis if you like, and I'll guarantee that it'll run to a quarter of a million words. By the time it's done there'll be more holes in this jerrymandered scheme than in all the colanders ever made "

"Do you have any alternative ideas?" asked Svenson.

Benbow felt the emotion slip away from him again. Mueller's reaction told him that both of them knew more than they had so far admitted. Wearily, he shook his head.

"I've only been here six months, Svenson. Mueller forecast a long time ago what would ultimately happen on Earth, and he was believed. He planned the operation which has resulted in this base. He created, he set it up, organized the supply lines and the evacuation. All the governments of Earth believed his prognosis and co-operated with him even while they were being dragged under by the tide of events." Benbow stood up and slammed a fist on the table before Mueller. "No one will ever convince me that he would overlook such a simple, plain fact as economic survival "

"You pay me too big a compliment, Peter," said Mueller

"Blast your platitudes "

The old eyes twinkled at him with misplaced humor.

"Svenson is making a routine trip tomorrow, so your—ah —accusations have come at an opportune moment Peter,

I think it would be a good idea if you went with him. Perhaps you will find some of the answers that you seek."

"Where to?" demanded Benbow.

Svenson chuckled maliciously. "To Diemos," he replied.

XIII

BENBOW HARDLY recalled getting back to his dormitory. The surprise engendered by Svenson's announcement was more than just surprise; there had been an element of shock about it that had jarred him far more than he would ever have admitted.

Diemos!

The outer and smaller of the two Martian satellites, it had a diameter of around five miles, and was so far out from the parent planet—over fourteen thousand miles—that it was quite invisible to the naked eye.

From what he knew of it, and from what he had learned since his arrival on Mars, Benbow had not even considered that it might have any use. The inner satellite, Phobos, was an entirely different matter. It was a natural space station, and its size—twice that of Diemos—made it an ideal storage place and anchorage for the ships from Earth and the smaller Mars-bound rockets.

But Diemos!

Even his sketchy knowledge did nothing to answer the questions that had risen in his mind, and he lay, tossing restlessly, until far into the Martian night.

When he awoke next morning there was an expectation within him that he had not known for a long time. His first waking thought was not—as it had always been before—of Drusilla, and when he did think of her later on, it was with a pang of regret that she could be so easily dismissed. Benbow felt as if he was on the verge of a great adventure, and that feeling continued all through the long day.

A tractor took Svenson and him to the rocket field that lay six miles off on the far side of the already familiar hill range. There were no drugs this time, and the rocket had a two man crew.

He lay strapped in his bunk and experienced all the

79

discomforts which he had heard about, and there was a recurrence of the disgusting vomiting that he had met with so soon after leaving Earth. This time he was conscious and prepared.

There was no sensation of landing or slowing down. Indeed, Benbow had dozed out of sheer boredom and was only warned of their arrival by the slight metallic clang as a flexible tunnel was connected to the main air lock of the rocket.

There was weightlessness, stark metal, discomfort. An antiseptic cleanliness about the polished metal and the gleaming suits of the men who greeted them at the other end of the tunnel. They passed through another air lock and beyond it there was solid rock, a mine shaft driven deep into the surface of the tiny satellite. There was air too, and the temperature was at least bearable so that they could discard the pressure suits.

Benbow noticed that there were men and women here, far more people altogether than he would have expected. The whole satellite close to the surface was tunneled and caverned to make living quarters, workshops, storage areas, far greater in scope and size than anything he had seen on Mars. He was introduced to many people during his progress through the man-made shafts and caverns, and always he noted Svenson's half humorous reference to him as being "Mueller's latest recruit."

He met two people that he had known many years before on Earth. There was a certain thrill in the contact, but that pleasure was soon wiped away by the stirring of memories that were painful to him and to them. They ate a meal in a large communal canteen, a strange meal because of the almost complete lack of gravity. They sat at tables anchored to the floor, and Benbow found the action of eating and drinking as uncomfortable as it had been on the ship that brought him from Earth. Even old skills had to be relearned.

Svenson showed him everything, explained everything that they saw with an offhand casualness that wasn't entirely lost on Benbow. The pièce de résistance was being saved until the end. Everything else was merely a preliminary.

They saw laboratories and machine shops, drawing offices

and design centers; there were tool makers and model makers and draughtsmen, and yet nowhere did Svenson give him any clue as to the end purpose of all the activity. Benbow watched engineers moving giant girders and metal sheets with one hand; he watched chemists solving problems without the aid of gravity, and realization came to him slowly.

As they stood on a high catwalk and looked down into a cavernous machine shop, he said to Svenson, "I should have remembered that two and two make four."

The Swede raised his eyebrows in the inevitable question.

"If I'd really thought about it," Benbow told him, "I would have realized that there just wasn't enough metal or chemicals or food or people on Mars. I just took it for granted that the sum total of people on Phobos and on Mars was around four thousand." He looked somberly at Svenson. "Is that what everyone thinks? Everyone who doesn't ask questions like me?"

"Yes, Peter," Svenson nodded. "We do not advertize our activity here. About half of all the material shipped from Earth finds its way here, to Diemos."

"Half?" Benbow was incredulous. "But—that means that the project here is as big as the base on Mars."

"It's bigger."

"Then why is it secret? If you have the answer here—"

"Peter, we can't." Svenson snapped the words with a sudden savagery that was quite out of character. "We can't —not yet."

He moved away along the catwalk and Benbow followed him more clumsily because he had not yet regained the ability to move under low gravity with any grace.

The Swede led him along a narrow, metal-lined corridor and up a short metal ladder. There was a hatchway open at the top and Benbow banged his shoulder painfully on the edge as he floated through it. They were in a small room with rough rock walls, and set in one of the walls was a large metal cover with two handles that showed it could be moved aside.

Svenson gestured to the panel. "There, God willing, lies the answer, Peter. If answer there be."

He crossed and threw his strength against the handles. The cover moved easily and rumbled aside to reveal a thick, entirely transparent window, three inches thick, set in the rock. Beyond it was the dark sky of deep space, the brilliant gleam of stars, the eternal canopy of the universe. Benbow moved nearer as Svenson gestured to him, and stopped dead in his tracks, bobbing ludicrously, completely off balance and shaken by what he saw.

Low down, nestling close to the surface of Diemos and held to it by a score or more of flexible tunnels, was a ship.

But it was a ship such as Benbow had never, in his wildest dreams, conceived of as a possibility. Its main bulk was hidden from him by the curve of the tiny satellite, but it put forth a thousand lights that gleamed and glittered and gave notice of a vast immensity that was out of range of his vision.

"That is our answer." Svenson's voice was a mere whisper, as if he, too, were overawed by what he saw, even though, for him, this could not have been the first time. "Eight years' work, Benbow, and another two years ahead of us. Then she'll be ready."

"Evacuation." It was the only word that came to mind. Benbow looked at the Swede. "Complete and final evacuation? That isn't an answer, Svenson, it's a dream created by an old man."

"Blast you!" Svenson slapped his hands together angrily. "Can't you see any further than the Solar System? In fifty years Earth will be a dead planet, and in half that time Mars, too, will be finished—if things go on as they are."

"Then how does this answer it all?"

"Two ships—that is one of them, the other is building on the far side of Diemos—each with a crew of two thousand. A holding party on Mars with supplies to last them a century. Twenty years to Alpha Centaurus, and twenty five to Sirius. We shall have two chances, and one of them must succeed."

Benbow was shaking his head from side to side like a metronome in denial of all he heard. "It's crazy—crazy. Svenson, you must be mad. Mueller must be mad—"

"Can't you see anything but the conventional answer? Can't you see that we have no choice? Earth is finished."

"I know that—"

"And Mars cannot supply the answer."

Benbow was dumb with an almost hysterical denial bubbling inside him.

"Then what other answer is there?" insisted Svenson.

Benbow turned away from the window; he felt physically sick with the enormity of the idea that had been thrust upon him.

"What about the people left on Mars?"

"We'll keep Phobos and the Terran space station manned and operating as long as possible. There will be expeditions to Earth, and with any luck they'll be able to get a flow of food and supplies out for a long time even if White Sands does go under. If we find a new world then we shall spend ten years settling in, and the ship will be sent back with a skeleton crew. That will be the end. The Solar System will die."

"What of Earth?"

Svenson shrugged. "Mueller reckons that it'll be five or six centuries at least before things start to get back to normal Remember, the whole ecology of the planet will be destroyed by the atmospheric and geologic changes that he has foreseen." Svenson hesitated. "One day, perhaps, we'll be able to send an expedition back."

"Is that all?" Benbow asked dully. "One day—perhaps?"

"What do you want us to do? Stay here and die? We can't do that, not while there is the slightest chance that the race can survive."

Benbow was rapidly regaining control of himself, and his thoughts were beginning to crystalize as the explanations filled in the gaps in his knowledge.

He said, "All right. Grant that this is the answer. Why keep it a secret?"

Svenson smiled coldly. "Because of reactions like yours. Because we have foreseen the psychological impact that such an idea would have if it became general knowledge. There are a thousand people here who know, and most of them—like you—figured it out for themselves. Some are here because they are indispensible, but all of them are adjusted to the idea and to the concepts that arise from that idea."

"But the people back on Earth—don't they know?" Benbow

turned back and looked at Svenson in sudden horror. "Svenson, they haven't been told!"

The Swede shook his head.

"But why?" Benbow pleaded. "Surely they, of all people, have a right to be told?"

"And if they were told, just how do you think the supplies would keep coming? How long would White Sands and Woomera last? How long would any sort of civilization have lasted on Earth if we had told them five years ago what we were planning?" Svenson shook his head. "You know the answer to that as well as I do. There would have been the biggest blowup since the coming of the Weed. Supplies would have stopped, we would have been accused of treason, of running off and abandoning Earth. They might even have sent an armed force to stop us."

Benbow's head was in a complete whirl; his composure, which had been reasserting itself, was lost once more under the weight of a nightmare from which he felt he should have awoken a long time ago.

"It's the only way, Peter," insisted Svenson. "We have to dangle the carrot before them. As long as they believe that the answer is here, on Mars, then they'll play along and do everything in their power to give us what we need—to give us a fighting chance of carrying on. But once tell them that Mars is no good, that we are clearing out to look for new worlds in other star systems," he paused significantly, "then, Peter, that is when the trouble will begin."

Tears pricked Benbow's eyes and his throat was choked with an anguish that was beyond belief. Drusilla, he thought, oh, God, Drusilla, what have I done to you?"

"Sleep on it." Svenson's voice was far off at the end of a long, echoing corridor. "Sleep on it, Peter, and when you have thought about we will talk again."

XIV

A DARK NIGHT of agony produced nothing save a chilling knot of depression. Benbow knew it was wrong—all of it—but he could not say why. Somehow, somewhere, Mueller had gone wrong; his ideas had swept away and beyond the bounds of reason and entered the realms of fantasy. Or was it simply that he, Benbow, was incapable of evaluating the situation in its entirety?

At breakfast he was greeted by a somber Svenson whose first word was a quizzical, "Well?"

"I don't know—I just don't know."

"Hardly the answer of the trained observer."

Benbow shrugged. "What use is a trained observer in a situation like this? All he observes is his own impending doom." He sucked hot coffee from a plastic bottle. "Someone once said that even on the most exalted throne in the world a man sits on nothing but his own backside."

"Montaigne, the essayist," said Svenson. "So what?"

"I wonder if Mueller has lost touch with reality, that's all."

"Or is it merely that you can't face the reality? That, too, is possible."

"I know it."

"I'm heading back to Mars today." Svenson studied the table before him. "Are you coming with me?"

Benbow chuckled coldly. "You mean will I keep my mouth shut about all this when we get back. Is that it?"

Svenson nodded, but he didn't look up.

"Yes," said Benbow. "Your secret is safe with me. It's safe because I can't fault it. I know instinctively that it's wrong, but I don't know why. When I do I'll go and tell Mueller first. Panic and revolution are the last thing that anyone wants now."

Svenson grinned. "If you can find another answer we'll be only too happy. Believe me, Peter, we don't want this. It smacks too much of cowardice in the face of the enemy."

"He who fights and runs away—?"

"Something like that."

"Before we leave," Benbow hesitated, "can I see one of the ships?"

The Swede laughed outright. "Already laid on. We're not leaving until later today so we'll have time to see at least a part of it."

Later, Benbow realized why Svenson had said, "part of it." He knew from his first sight through the thick window that the vessel was immense beyond any imagination that he might have had, but the sheer, cold complexity of it came to him only as he walked within its seemingly boundless hull. There were long corridors, vast storage spaces, control rooms, engine rooms, play rooms, whole factories and machine shops, wide areas of hydroponic gardens. He saw hospitals, libraries, nurseries, two complete schools, three auditoriums, lecture halls, assembly rooms, laboratories, dormitories, married quarters. Everything had been thought of, everything taken into account.

And when it was ended he hadn't seen half.

There were water storage tanks, oxygenation plants, synthetic food plants, and one vast area where small herds of sheep and pigs could be raised.

"We're getting a dozen of each shipped from Earth," said Svenson. "Cows are out, but we're thinking of a few dozen chickens."

"Gravity will be against you," Benbow told him. "Normal gestation of animals and humans can be seriously disrupted without normal gravity."

"We've thought about it. Once clear of the Solar System and in deep space we shall be able to rotate the ship on its axis. Oh, it won't be Terran normal, we know that, but we reckon it will be enough to offset the worst effects. The living quarters will be against the outer rim where the greatest effect of centrifugal force will be felt."

It might work, thought Benbow. It just might work. He felt awe deep within him that so much had been done with so few resources. He felt as he had done that day so many months before at White Sands when he had first seen the forests of gantries and listened to the merciless clamor of men and machines. This was Mankind fighting back; this was the terrible singlemindedness of a race who didn't know when it was licked.

Perhaps that was what was wrong? Perhaps he knew that he was beaten; perhaps that was why he didn't see a future in this—this grand evacuation. And yet—!

And yet, he wasn't convinced. He knew that Svenson expected him to be—that was the whole point of the tour. He was supposed to be overawed, bludgeoned into acceptance by the sheer size and scope of all that he saw within the great vessel. That he was not completely overawed

86

was surprising. He should have been, and indeed there were times during the tour when he felt it; but always at the back of his mind a small voice kept nagging at him. It was wrong; it wouldn't work; Mueller had miscalculated.

He was able, quite sincerely, to voice his wonder at all that he saw; he could appreciate all that had been done; he could relate the end product to the years of toil, of making do, of stretching out the materials at hand so that there was no waste. There were myriads of problems that had been solved—were still being solved, and all of them were being done by a few hundred men and women who relied on a thin, tenuous thread that stretched back for millions of miles to a dying, tortured world.

And that, he knew, was the true wonder of it all; therein lay the bright hope of Mueller and Svenson and the rest. It lay in achieving the impossible, and that, Benbow thought, was where they had gone wrong. The aim was overshadowed by the path they wished to tread in reaching that aim. The great ships were not the means—they were the end.

He thought about it all the rest of that day, and he thought about it during the journey back to Mars. He could not reach a final conclusion. Who was he to say that they were wrong? They had more facts than he did, and if it was wrong to attempt the impossible, then Mankind had been wrong for many, many centuries. Yet even this introspection did not help to convince him. He knew, deep within himself, that it was wrong because it smelled wrong. His scientist's intuition—that inner eye which men of science deny out loud, yet which they privately admit is so important—told him that Mueller wasn't on the right path. And if Mueller had strayed then his disciples had strayed with him.

They rode back from the rocket landing ground in the closed sand tractor and Benbow's silence over the past hours had not been lost on Svenson. They drew near to the great airlock that gave entrance to the main dome, and he said quietly, "Have you thought enough, Benbow?"

Benbow pursed his lips and looked out of the window at the bulbous, alien growth that spawned upon the red sands of Mars.

"No," he replied softly. "No, I haven't thought one half enough for you or for myself. But you needn't worry. I'll keep my silence as I have promised."

Svenson smiled and nodded.

The tractor rolled through the airlock and pulled to a halt in the main parking area—a hard-packed area of sand just inside the dome.

As they alighted Svenson said, "We'll go straight along and see Mueller. He'll be keen to know your reactions."

"He may not be when he knows what they are."

"I think he will respect you for them."

They walked along the narrow paths that led between the shabby, weatherboard huts. Under the protection of the dome only the flimsiest of building materials were needed, and it was this impermanence that made the Martian Project such a ramshackle and dejected place.

As he looked at it, after even such a short break as this, Benbow was shocked by what he saw.

They reached Mueller's hut and went inside. The old man was not there, but as they turned to leave a woman came out of an adjoining office. Benbow recognized her as Mueller's aide, Nancy something-or-other. He felt ashamed that he could not identify her more readily.

"I heard that you had landed, Doctor Svenson." Her smile embraced Benbow as well. "Professor Mueller has gone to the radio room. He doesn't know that you have come back, though I did warn him this morning that you were on your way."

"Trouble?" Svenson snapped the word out with the air of a man who could smell it from a great distance.

Her smile wavered and her eyes dropped, drifting away from them.

"White Sands hasn't been able to raise Woomera for three days. That's all I know."

Benbow felt his stomach turn over and a dead weight lay across it as if he had received a heavy blow.

"My God!" Svenson whispered. He turned and left the office at a dead run, and Benbow followed, not because he wanted to, but because he had to know as well. The same ache gnawed at him that he had known before on far too many occasions, and he recognized it for what it was, the anticipatory pain that preceded another disaster.

The radio room was a single hut in the neighboring dome, a small one that held the technical equipment, the radar, the wireless, the television hookup with Phobos. They reached it through a tunnel dug beneath the sand and plugged by airtight doors that were always kept closed. That way, damage to one dome could not affect the other.

Svenson wrenched at the first door, tearing at the catches with a desperation that communicated itself to Benbow. If Woomera had indeed been overwhelmed then it meant that White Sands was alone. If that was so their supply route to Earth was hanging by the slenderest of threads.

The concrete floor of the short tunnel rang beneath their feet, and then they were through the second door, slamming it shut behind them. They climbed the few short steps to ground level and Svenson halted abruptly.

From the radio hut, his shoulders bent, came Mueller— a Mueller who had aged twenty years. His grotesque wireframed spectacles were askew on his round button nose, but they were no longer funny. They were tragic, the tragicomedy of a clown who knew that the show was over for good and all.

He came up to them slowly, and as he saw them he tried to walk a little straighter, he tried to smile but the effort was a pathetic mockery.

"Svenson, Benbow. I heard that you were on the way back."

"What has happened, Mueller?" rasped the Swede. "Nancy said that Woomera—"

"Is finished—gone." Mueller's voice was a dry whisper that rattled in the still air of the dome. "White Sands got a reconnaissance plane over there yesterday. It was fired on when it tried to land."

Benbow sat down weakly on the small wall beside the steps leading down to the tunnel.

"Are they sure?" insisted Svenson.

Mueller nodded. "Yes." He took off his glasses and wiped his hand across his eyes. "Yes, they are sure."

"So," Svenson relaxed visibly. "So, White Sands is on its own now."

"There is more."

Benbow looked at Mueller and realized that there had to be more. Woomera had been hanging by a thread for too long for news of its sudden overthrow to be such a surprise. A matter of regret, yes. A matter for mourning such as this—no!

"Well?" He hardly recognized the voice which issued from his dry, constricted throat.

The rheumy old eyes looked at him and there were tears in them. Softly, Mueller said, "The earthquakes are beginning, and the volcanoes are being born. What I foresaw all those years ago has come to pass. I fear that the final dissolution of Earth has begun."

XV

THEY WALKED back through the tunnel to Mueller's office in deathly silence. A pall of agony darkened everything around them, and Benbow felt his limbs trembling with shock as he walked behind Svenson. It was an indescribable feeling. He felt that he was experiencing an emotion that no man had ever known before; a nadir of hopelessness, of bewilderment, of dejection; a catharsis of death—yet more than death, if such a thing could be possible.

Mueller's secretary met them at the door.

"Is it—true?"

Mueller nodded and passed inside, and as he followed Benbow could see twin tears forming rivulets in the ashen cheeks of the woman. There was nothing he could say, nothing he could do.

The office had an air of abandonment. The paper-littered desk, the chair behind it askew—evidence of Mueller's hurried departure—the filing cabinet with one drawer half open. Benbow and Svenson stood before the desk and Mueller sat behind it, his chair turned away from them so that he could look out of the window. The Swede pushed the drawer of the filing cabinet shut and leaned against it, his eyes fixed firmly on the floor. Benbow sank shakily into the single chair.

The silence drew out interminably as they stood or sat,

each locked with his thoughts, his own private grief. Mueller's chair creaked as he stood up and looked out of the window, and Benbow heard him sob once, brokenly. Svenson lifted his great, blond head and looked at the old man, then he, too, crossed to stand beside Mueller.

"Oh, God!" The words were dragged from him, in a great, shuddering whisper, and he turned away with lowered head.

Benbow felt a twinge of alarm over all the other emotion that tore at his being. He crossed to where Mueller stood and looked out of the window. There, on the red sand, gathering slowly and quietly, the men and women of the base stood looking blankly and hopelessly at the small hut that was Mueller's headquarters.

"The news is spreading," said Mueller huskily.

More people were arriving by the minute, and they stood mutely, horribly silent, save here and there where a woman pressed a handkerchief to her lips and eyes.

"What do they want of me?" whispered Mueller. "In heaven's name, what do they want of me?"

"Comfort," rasped Benbow, horrified at the loudness of his voice. "You're the father figure now, Mueller. They're like children who have lost their way. They want you to tell them what to do."

Mueller shook his head from side to side in wordless agony.

"Have you any answer?" asked Benbow.

"No, Peter, not the answer they want. They want me to tell them that things are not as bad as they think. They want hope, and I cannot offer them one tiny piece of that."

"Tell them about the ships," rasped Benbow. "Tell them about your great evacuation, your master plan for survival." He felt an unreasoning, unreasonable anger rising within him. "Go on, Mueller, you've got all the answers. Tell them as you told me. See if they'll swallow it as all those others have done. Ask them how they feel about abandoning Earth altogether. Convince them that it's the only way—"

"Benbow, stop it." Svenson's voice cut across his tirade like a knife, bitter and acid in its savagery.

The passion drained from him and he sank weakly back into his chair. "I'm sorry."

Mueller looked at him sadly, but there was understanding in his eyes. "I know, Peter. We're all facing something that no man has ever faced before. Pray heaven that no man ever will again." He turned his chair away from the silent crowd, shutting them out as effectively as if there had been curtains to be drawn.

"I forgot to ask you about your trip, Peter," he said. "From your comments I think that perhaps you do not agree with my solution."

"No, I don't. It just isn't the answer, Mueller."

"Why not?"

"I don't know. I wish I did. There's something wrong about it—something I can't put my finger on. Oh, I know," he waved away Mueller's attempted interruption, "Mars isn't the answer either, I agree. We might hang on here for a hundred years—perhaps longer—but in the end the system would collapse for lack of support from Earth."

"Go on."

Benbow shrugged. "What else is there? Svenson tells me that you hope to leave a holding party here, on Mars, for up to fifty years. Do you honestly think that any group will last that long? Of course they won't and you know it."

"They might."

"And they might not. Dammit, Mueller, would you live here for the rest of your life under these domes with disaster threatening you every hour of every day? Would you raise a family in the hope that they'll carry on where you left off, waiting for a ship that may never come? A ship that may never find the El Dorado which it seeks out there among the stars?" He shook his head. "You wouldn't and I wouldn't, and I don't think any of those people outside that window would do it either."

"I shall," said Mueller mildly. "I am too old to embark on a mission such as I have planned, Peter." He chuckled sadly. "Those that stay will need a father figure to lead them. I think I may be able to provide that image during the first difficult years. After that, things will settle into a routine."

"I can't convince you, can I?"

"No." Mueller shook his head. "I have lived with this thing from the beginning. I have spent thousands of hours over hundreds of long, dark nights thinking about it, searching for an alternative. If there was one to be found I think I would have found it—I, or someone else. But there isn't any alternative. These ships, they are—what do you say?—a long shot, yes, a long shot, but they are all that we have."

Benbow turned away and clasped his hands together before his face in an agony of denial. "There is something, something! Mueller, there has to be."

"Then it will have to be found quickly. We have no time left to us, Peter. Every day, every hour, the curtain is being drawn against us. We are living on the edge of a precipice. Any moment the ledge may give way."

Carefully, Benbow said, "Are you sure that you are not being blinded by the path you wish to tread, so blinded that the goal itself has become blurred?"

Mueller said nothing.

"What in hell does that mean?" demended Svenson.

"How long have you both been working on this ship building project? You Mueller? Six—eight years?" Benbow looked at them grimly. "How long is it since you even considered another answer? Oh, I know, those ships represent the greatest feat of engineering ever undertaken by Mankind. With the resources at your disposal you've done a wonderful thing."

"Get to the point," said Svenson.

"All right. Those ships will do what you want. They'll take you out of the Solar System and across space to Alpha Centauras and Sirius. And then what?" Benbow leaned forward in his chair. "Mueller, you don't even know if those two stars have any planets."

"Centaurus has two that we know about. The Russians spotted them with their space station telescope twelve years ago," replied Mueller.

"And to be spotted they must be pretty large. That telescope was only a thirty-inch job. I was going to say that you don't even know if the two stars have planets which are habitable. It's a long chance that they have—and you know it."

"But still, there is a chance."

"And if it doesn't come off?"

Mueller dropped his eyes from Benbow's stark gaze. He

93

took off his ridiculous wire-framed spectacles and began to polish one of the lenses on his shirt sleeve

"It is a possibility which is hard to consider."

"Oh, Mueller, come off it!"

"Stop baiting him, Benbow," broke in Svenson angrily, "I warned you—"

"No, Arne," said Mueller. "It's all right." His voice was tired and infinitely old. "Peter, you are a clever man. The months you have been with us have proved that. You have thought about this thing and you have come up with questions that have not been framed by one in a hundred of the people who came here before you."

"You haven't answered my question."

Mueller sighed and replaced his glasses. "I have thought about it often in the past, and I have decided on the answer. No one knows it but myself—not even Svenson." He smiled wryly at the Swede. "If—mark you, Peter—if there is nothing for us there, then the ships will go on."

"What?"

"They will head for the next star, and the next, and the next, for as long as they can survive."

"It's madness," breathed Benbow.

Mueller slammed a hand down on the table top in a sudden flurry of passion that was quite out of character. "It is all madness. For fifteen years there has been nothing but madness, and we have all lived through it. Only madness can help us survive—oh, not I, not you, but the human race."

Benbow looked at Svenson. The Swede was staring grimly at the old man seated behind the table.

"Do you go along with this, Svenson?"

"Yes, I have thought about it, and this is the answer that I have come to also. There would be no point in turning back. There would be nothing to come back for."

Benbow slumped in his chair and buried his face in his hands. If one accepted the logic of the ships, in the first place then one had to accept the logic of this latest revelation. All the energy of the Mars base had gone into the building of those ships, it had been focused on one great dream, one chance that might be the answer, the salvation of Mankind.

And somewhere, somehow, it had gone wrong.

"I have been thinking," said Mueller softly, and there was no trace now of the emotion he had shown bare minutes before. "Since we heard from White Sands, I have been thinking."

Benbow shifted uneasily and looked up.

"Now that Woomera is gone—now that the seismic conditions which I foresaw have begun, it means that our supplies will be greatly reduced. We shall not feel the effects for about six months, but we have to act now in preparation for the fall of White Sands."

"What shall we do?" asked Svenson.

"Concentrate our efforts." The old man looked at them bleakly. "We shall have to put far more into the ships than we had planned. It will mean less effort here, on Mars. I believe that we must get those ships away within a year and a half Earth time—or they will never get away at all."

XVI

THE DAYS FLED into weeks, the weeks into months. Benbow worked with all the rest, hard, relentless work of all kinds. He was a biologist, a chemist, a cook on occasion, a carpenter. He drove sand tractors, he hauled equipment, he held tools for experienced engineers. He made two more trips to Diemos—and he wrestled with his thoughts.

He watched the grim, gray faces of the men and women, saw the quiet desperation with which they worked. He saw their despondency as the supply rockets from Phobos carried less and less food and materials. Supplies for the main base were, in truth, being cut to the bone. The erection of another dome to provide more living space was abandoned, and with that decision everyone knew that the noose was being drawn a little tighter.

From White Sands the rockets to the space station beyond Earth's atmosphere took off only once in three days, and they carried more materials than they did men.

The Canadian granaries had fallen into chaos and confusion, and only the wide plains of the American mid-west were still under any sort of control. The shrinking world of Man fell deeper into a morass of destruction and ruin. White Sands itself held on only because of the determination and the discipline of the military forces controlling the area, and they were so hardpressed that they could only hold the boundaries which they had set themselves after Canada had gone under. They had little time to explore the rest of the planet, and such news as they came by was garnered from small groups who fought their way through to reach the one place where civilization still ruled. A few scout planes made long distance reconnaissance flights, but they could not land anywhere in safety and such details as they brought back were gained from a low height and traveling at four hundred miles an hour.

The tales brought back by the planes, and told by the few survivors who reached White Sands, told harrowing tales of the earthquekes which had begun to shake the planet; of the volcanoes that erupted in places where no volcanoes had been known before. What was left of New York after riot and revolution had slid beneath the weed-clogged sea in a quake that had rocked the whole eastern seaboard of the American continent. The feudal states of northern India had been racked by the lifting mass of a newborn range of volcanic hills, and the whole Mediterranean area of Europe and Africa was a volcanic waste which poured forth yellow clouds of poisonous sulphur. Japan was gone entirely, and beneath the rolling mists of the former Pacific ocean newborn islands raised fiery peaks towards dark and boiling skies.

A long range survey jet reported dark, bare rocks on Greenland—the first time in thousands of years that they had not been covered by snow and ice. Through gaps in the mists the red flames turned the icy north into a hellish, volcanic land of chaos and destruction.

From England there was nothing.

For Benbow the scattered news from Earth held no interest. He shut it from his mind and paid attention only to those problems which concerned him from day to day. There was nothing for him on Earth—nothing that he wished to think about.

Most of the people reaching them now were Americans,

though there was still a sprinkling of Australians and Europeans who'd got away from Woomera before the final collapse. The thin trickle of people from England had long since dried up.

For that Benbow was thankful. It meant that he could stop the hopeless, pointless, inevitable questions that he was forced to ask. He knew that he was an object of pity every time he went hesitantly to a newcomer; he knew that he would learn nothing of Drusilla, yet he was drawn like an automaton in a futile charade of question and negation. In the end, he had not even felt anguish or despair; there was only a dull acceptance of the inevitable.

There was time, at last, only to work and to eat and to sleep—there was room for nothing else.

Most of his work was in the laboratory under the rapidly diminishing supervision of Martha Dresden. Martha seemed to have become even thinner—a fact which he would have thought was quite impossible—and her parchment face took on a waxy, yellowish tint that was almost corpselike. She spent more and more time with her children, fawning on them like a wild animal whose cubs are threatened; and this suited Benbow. He had almost free run of the laboratory and his work there was only interrupted by such other duties as were necessary.

Larson visited him often. The big Negro had, somehow, retained his easy-going, unworried attitude, and he treated Benbow with a complete and therapeutic lack of pity. Every day on Mars was like every day on Earth—before the Weed —that was Larson's philosophy. He hummed his spirituals and lived for the day; tomorrow was too far off to be bothered with.

He came to Benbow one evening as the deep purple sky was drawing into blackness, and he stood in the lab leaning against one of the benches while Benbow worked at a microscope. He hummed his spiritual and said nothing.

Benbow glanced up from his work and saw him there, his eyes fixed on the ground, his thick lips moving slightly as he sang.

"For heaven's sake, you're the sorriest looking man I ever did see."

Larson raised his eyes and looked sadly at Benbow. "A new group got in from Earth today, Peter."

"I know." Benbow bent to his work again. "I heard the rocket land about three hours ago."

Larson hummed tunelessly to himself for a second. "They're over with Mueller now."

"So?"

"One of them was asking for you."

Benbow stiffened, the slide he was examining swam in his vision for a second before he lifted his head. Oh, God, he thought, not now—now after all this time.

"I thought I'd better come over and warn you, boy."

Benbow licked his lips, and tried to control his shivering nerves.

"Do you—" he swalled a dry lump that had gathered in his throat. "Do you know his name?"

"No." Larson shook his head. "But he's a limey, that's for sure. First thing he asked about was you."

The ache deepened within Benbow, the tight knot in his stomach that he had fought against for so long was back, the pain was more intense than it had ever been before. No door could open now, not when he had buried everything— or thought he had buried it. His palms were moist and his hands shook slightly as he wiped them down the front of his shirt.

"Maybe he's got some news for you, Peter," said Larson.

"Blast you, Larson. I don't want any news. Can't you understand that? It's gone—lost—forgotten. I buried it here, on Mars, along with all the other things, with all the other memories. It's dead." He looked out at the dark sky with the stars that were hazed by the thin coverlet of the dome.

"Sometimes things aren't dead, Peter. We only think they are—we wish them to be."

"I know."

"I left my wife and two kids dead in a burning house." Larson spoke coldly, without inflection. "Some looters got at them while I was out scavenging."

Benbow looked up slowly. It was the first time the Negro had ever mentioned his former life.

"You see, we've all got something."

"But yours is really dead. There's no uncertainty about it. With Drusilla—" He stopped. It was the first time in many weeks that her name had passed his lips. Who was the man with Mueller?

He heard the outer door of the lab click open, and there were footsteps in the short corridor outside. His mouth was dry and he felt sick with apprehension; the seconds seemed interminable as the footsteps faltered uncertainly.

Larson called, "In here," and the door opened slowly.

The short, wiry form of Hector Ball stepped hesitantly into view. His moon face was thinner than Benbow remembered, and the gray eyes bore a haunted, weary look that made him old beyond his years.

"Hector!"

"Hello, Peter."

They shook hands gravely and calmly, each appraising the other, each disappointed at what he saw. The long months since last they met had taken their toll.

Ball said, "You look well, Peter—a little older . . ."

Benbow laughed coldly. "The platitudes can keep, Hector. Larson here tells me that your first questions were of me. After all this time—me?"

"You're the only one that I knew for sure was here—on Mars," smiled Ball. "After all, it wasn't exactly well publicized."

"Who told you."

"Drusilla."

So there it was, out in the open, stark and naked, terrible in its resurrection. The open grave of his emotions lay before him as if it had never been closed; the pain, the desperation, the longing, all were there as he had known them before in all their awful clarity.

He sat down on the high lab stool, aware that he was shivering uncontrollably. Larson turned and left the room as silently as if he had never been, and Ball stood quiet and waited for the question that both of them knew must come.

"What happened?"

"We knew about the opposition to Quince," Ball told him. "Hillary was asked to join in the uprising because of his

99

group of marines. He pretended to fall in with them, but he tipped me off and I warned Quince."

"But if Quince knew—?"

"He knew that there wasn't much he could do. He knew that the end was near, and I think he was glad. I remember, he laughed when I told him. He said how stupid it was—a pack of angry dogs fighting over a cast-off shoe." Ball sat down beside Benbow. "One last plane got away to America before the collapse, and he sent those people whom he thought would be most valuable to the Mars project. God knows there were few enough of us."

"You were one of them?"

Ball nodded. "He wanted to keep his promise to you, but Drusilla couldn't make it." His eyes were haunted and pitiful as he met Benbow's stark gaze. "The baby was due any time. The plane wasn't pressurized. It could have killed them both."

Benbow looked away, the ache within him deeper than the blackest void of space.

"Hillary promised to take care of her—"

"Hillary?"

"There was a hovercraft—a big one—that Quince kept for emergency. It could take twenty people, twenty-four at a pinch. Quince decided that Hillary should take it and get clear with a few women and a handful of marines. They were to head south, get across the Channel, and keep going until they reached North Africa. Then they were to follow the coast until they reached Freetown, and head southwest across the Atlantic until they hit Pernambuco—"

"They'd never make it. What about fuel?"

"Scavenge for it. Quince reckoned they'd have a chance if they made the Atlantic crossing."

"Better if they'd headed north to Iceland and across to Greenland and Canada."

"There wasn't any promise of fuel. The hovercraft had a range of two thousand miles fully loaded, and that meant they had to go to places where there were refineries." Ball paused. Then he said, "I—I was at White Sands over four months, Peter. There was never any news."

The silence dragged out interminably.

Benbow said, "They may never have got clear."

"I think they did. Quince had it all laid on. He knew the time and the day when the revolt was due—thanks to Hillary—and he planned to get the hovercraft away during the night previously. There wasn't any reason why things should go wrong, and we do know that the revolt happened just as Hillary said it would."

Benbow bowed his head in his hands. The door had slammed shut again with all the viciousness of an animal trap, but it had left him wide open to all those things that he had thought were buried. Oh, he couldn't blame Ball. The fault lay in his own accursed emotions; they leaked like a tap with a faulty washer, and the tighter the tap was turned the more water seemed to pour through.

"I'm sorry," said Ball huskily. He pushed the chair back and the wooden legs scraped the floor. Benbow heard a rustle of paper, and then the door closed and Ball was gone. He lifted his head and saw, on the desk before him, a crumpled envelope that had once been white.

The wording on it was faded but clear. It spoke his name, and the writing was Drusilla's.

XVII

EMOTIONS CANNOT be killed until the mind that bears them is itself destroyed. They can be buried deep, and they can remain buried until something happens to revive them, and when they are reborn they will blossom with a violence that is paralysing to the person who owns them.

So it was with Benbow.

The letter unlocked a barrier erected by his mind that he thought could never be breeched; and once it was shattered the tide that poured through was a molten river of pain that racked and crucified him with a suffering that was greater than any he had ever known before.

Drusilla spoke of her love and her hope, her eagerness for the child which was now—as she wrote the letters—only a few days from its birth. She was calmer now, she said, than ever in her life before. Ball and Hillary had watched over her like a pair of anxious cockerels, and Quince had promised that, whatever happened, he would see that she was safe. She begged him not to worry about her, he would have enough problems to deal with. If she could bring his child to him then she would do it. If not— well, he could rest easy in the knowledge that she would guard it and cherish it against the day when he would return to Earth. If all went well she might yet join him. In the meanwhile this letter would have to be a poor substitute. Should all else fail then she would try and get to Africa— to O'Brien. She knew the Butere area well; it was a quiet spot a long way from the troubled coastal plains, and she knew that O'Brien was well respected by the tribes in the area. Africa had been her home and she understood it even though it was so torn and troubled.

She ended with her love, her regret that she could not be with him just yet, her hope that all was well with him. . . .

Benbow sat for a long time while the echoes of her voice and her words eddied through him. Tears should have been born, but there were none; he was shocked, stricken with an ague that shook his muscles and his limbs, but his sobs were dry and racked with longing. Slowly, his emotions quieted and his mind regained control. The letter lay on the desk top before him, a single, crumbled sheet that carried all his past and all his future, a whisper from across a vast ocean of space and time.

If it lived his child would be eighteen months old by now.

It was quite dark when he left the laboratory. The base was quiet, work for the day had ended and there was food to be had, an hour or two of relaxation and talk before sleep. He walked across the hard-packed sand to the wall of the dome and stood for a long time looking through into the blackness beyond. The stars were brilliant and he could make out the shadow of the low hill range away in the distance.

How long he stood there he didn't know. It was a quiet oasis away from Ball and Larson and Mueller—away from all the others who would, by now, have learned what had happened. While he stayed there he would not have to meet their questioning glances; he would not need to endure their pity—reborn because Ball had come late upon the scene. Why should he be singled out? Everyone had some

102

personal grief buried deep within him; like Larson and his murdered family, or Martha Dresden and her dead child buried in the Martian sands beyond the dome.

He turned abruptly away from the dome wall. Some instinct told him what he had to do, and he realized that it was something that he should have done before. He went straight to the hut where Svenson had his sleeping quarters and found the Swede stretched out on his cot reading.

"Hello, Peter." Svenson swung his legs to the floor and sat up. "Are you all right?"

"You've heard about my visitor."

"Sure, everyone knows about—" He paused.

"The letter?" Benbow finished. "Svenson, I want to see Mueller."

"So?" The Swede's eyebrows raised in surprise. "You don't need my permission."

"I know that. I want you to be there."

"All right. Now is as good a time as any."

They left the hut and walked across to Mueller's sanctum. Svenson asked no questions and the short walk was made in utter silence. The old man sat, as ever, behind his littered desk, and, not for the first time, Benbow marveled that there should be so much paperwork on Mars.

"Peter. Arne." The old eyes were sympathetic over the top of the steel rimmed glasses, but Mueller made no mention of Ball.

"Don't you ever sleep?" asked Benbow.

Mueller shrugged. "Sleep is for the dead. I shall have an eternity of sleep. What can I do for you, Peter?"

"Quite a lot. I asked Svenson to be here because I think he should know what I have in my mind." He caught the glance that flickered between the two men. "Mueller, I have had a great deal to think about these last hours. You know about Ball—about the letter he brought me?"

Mueller nodded.

"Well, it helped me to make a decision that I should have made a long time ago." He hesitated, uncertain how to go on."

"The ships on Diemos?" asked Mueller.

"No, not about the ships."

Mueller was looking at him steadily, quite unconcerned,

almost as if he knew already what was in Benbow's mind.

"You'll probably think I'm crazy—"

Mueller chuckled softly.

"—but I've decided that I want to go back to Earth."

If he had thrown a bomb into the center of the room he could have had no greater effect on Svenson. The big Swede gaped at him with an amazement that was beyond description. His bulging eyes and gaping mouth were the cartoonist's parody of astonishment.

"You're mad!"

Mueller said nothing. Not a muscle of his face had changed, only the eyes showed an ineffable sadness.

"It could be arranged quite easily," said Benbow, hurrying into his explanations before Svenson could recover. "I could go back as a crew member to the space station and take my chance from there. There are some rockets heading back down to Earth—to White Sands—it shouldn't prove too hard."

"Mueller," Svenson leaned on the desk, "tell him he's mad."

"I can't do that, Arne," the old man replied quietly. "I don't believe he is. This, I expected. I am an old man, and I have seen too much of people and their reactions. When I heard about the letter that Doctor Ball brought with him, this is what I expected."

"You aren't surprised?" asked Benbow.

"No."

"Even if it were possible," snapped Svenson, "we couldn't allow it to happen."

"Why not?" demanded Benbow.

"Because of the ships. If you got back and blabbed about them and about our plans for them, there'd be hell to pay."

"You think I'm some sort of saboteur?" Benbow demanded angrily. "Dammit, Svenson, it'll take me all of six months or more before I get back, and by the time any action can be taken that might affect you those ships will be as ready as they'll ever be. Mueller, do you think I'd do anything to harm this project?"

"No, I don't."

"But can we risk it?" Svenson's face was red with passion.

104

"It would still mean trouble for the base that we intend leaving here. That would mean trouble for you, Heinz, and all who stay with you."

Mueller said nothing.

"Look," persisted Svenson, "it's just possible that White Sands can hang on longer than we think, and that will mean more material and more supplies for a period after the ships have left. It could mean the difference between life and death for the base."

Wearily, Benbow said, "Svenson, how many more times? I'm not a saboteur. I think you're wrong about the ships. I don't think they are the answer, but I won't do anything that's likely to endanger this whole project. Mueller knows why I've made this decision. It has nothing to do with your plans for evacuation. I don't think my presence here on Mars can offer anything more than I have already contributed. That letter given to me by Ball only confirmed what I have thought for a long time. I should never have left Earth in the first place."

"You didn't know all the facts at that time," said Mueller, "otherwise you might not have done."

"No," agreed Benbow, "I don't believe I would."

Svenson straightened from his posture against the desk. His lips were compressed in a taut line, and his blue eyes were etched with uncertainty. Clearly, he was not convinced, and for that Benbow could not blame him.

"Well, Mueller?" Benbow looked at the old man. It was he who counted, not Svenson; it was Mueller who would make the decision, and the Swede would bow to it even though he might disagree.

"You realize the difficulties?" asked Mueller gravely. "You will get to the satellite all right. But after that—"

"I have thought about it and I have to try."

"White Sands may be gone before you arrive. There will be only a return trip to Mars."

"I ran away once before," said Benbow. "I came here believing that I had something to contribute, but I know now that I haven't. The only thing left to me is to try and go back and do what I can—what I should have done before."

"That will be little enough," said Svenson.

Benbow shrugged. He knew it, but the knowledge was useless—as useless as he was here on Mars.

Mueller stirred and rose stiffly from his chair. "Go away and sleep, Peter," he said. "I will arrange it as you wish."

XVIII

It took almost four Terran weeks to arrange. Mueller decided that they should not advertise his decision, and when the time came for him to leave for Phobos, Benbow said a quiet farewell only to Ball, Larson, Svenson and Mueller.

His only real regret was in knowing that he would not see the old man again. Mueller still bore the mark of genius, and Benbow knew that he would not meet his like again.

His going was marred by the death, two days before his departure, of Martha Dresden. She died quietly in her bed for no other reason than that she no longer wished to live. Chen Su found her in the morning and her face bore a peace that it had never held in life.

It was two years almost to the day since Benbow arrived on Mars. He left—as he had come—with nothing. There was a vacuum in his life, a gap that would never be filled, and he was aware of a feeling that all of it—the base, the ships, everything—was a monstrous waste of the fading powers of Earth.

He spent the return journey cooking and cleaning for the other crew members. The great vessel traveled empty and there was nothing to do except work and sleep and eat. Benbow learned to walk on the outer hull of the ship, his magnetic boots forming the slender thread that held him fast. He learned of the crushing weight of agoraphobia— the spaceman's fear that grew outside the confines of the ship. He realized the tension that the crews of the supply ships lived under, and he marveled that they could survive it for journey after journey.

On the trip from Earth everything had been too new, too strange; he had been one of a large group making its first great voyage. This time it was so very different. The crew was small and blasé; the ship was empty; tempers frayed easily; there was the constant threat of danger.

But the time passed—slowly!

Benbow watched the light that was Earth grow in size from a pinpoint to a pea, from a pea to an orange. And the wonder of it was, as he stood on the deck of the space station and looked down, that Earth looked calm and serene, a blue globe that filled the whole of his vision. The atmospheric halo seemed undisturbed by the growing miasma of Weed and volcano. True, the continents were hazed, their coastlines dimmed by fog and cloud formations. There was a heavy concentration blotting out the entire Mediterranean area, and another covering the western half of the Pacific. North America, South America and the eastern Pacific were not visible to him as he watched, but Africa was clear and bright to the left of center.

It beckoned him and filled him with an emptiness and a despair that seemed to have no bottom. Africa was half a world away from White Sands.

Getting to White Sands proved the least of his worries. The commander of the station, a Frenchman named Duclos, wasn't keen on having him around too long. The monthly communication rocket was due thirty-nine hours after Benbow arrived, and it was on this that he traveled back to Earth.

On July the eighth one thousand nine hundred and eighty eight, Peter Benbow set foot once more on his native planet.

The landing area at White Sands was a small field twenty miles away from the main rocket building center, and away from the desert which was the main launching point for the supply rockets. The landing area was manned only temporarily and when the occasion demanded it.

Benbow stepped from the rocket and onto the elevator that would take him down to the ground. The two crewmen were with him, and he felt conscious of a semi-hysterical tremble as he breathed again the clean, fresh air of Earth. In the background the taint of sulphur lay musk-like, but his nostrils remembered more than he would have credited. They remembered the smell of grass and of trees;

there was the blown scent of flowers that bloomed wild around the edge of the landing field away from the scorched and blasted concrete of the main pad; he recalled the difference between this air and the canned, synthetic, purified pap that he had breathed for so long. It had been sterile, but until now he hadn't realized it.

A ground car waited for them on the edge of the field, and in minutes they were whirled away along dusty, broken roads between overgrown fields and weed filled ditches. It wasn't far off noon and the sun was hot and high. The open car brought cool breezes to Benbow's face, but he could feel the prickle of perspiration at his armpits and around his middle.

They passed through two small towns with wide, main streets in which people walked or sat or stood. People of the sort that he had not seen for—he couldn't remember how long. Machakos hadn't been like this, nor had Buxton; the Mars base had been like a beleaguered garrison; Phobos and Diemos the outposts of a dying civilization. These two towns were like throwbacks to another world, and only the armed soldiers, walking in pairs or lounging on street corners, told him that this was part of an area that lived only by martial law. The life of the communities had probably changed little over forty years—save that the soldiers had come.

Between the towns were large tracts of heavy cultivation, grain crops that caught the eye at once because of their midsummer ripeness; there were orchards and farms; cattle grazed in lush pastures. All of it filled Benbow and satisfied him in a manner he would not have dreamed possible. He hadn't known how much he had missed; he hadn't realized what it would really be like. On Mars his thoughts had been filled with the grinding necessity to survive, and when he had thought about Earth those thoughts had been clouded by thoughts of Drusilla. Now that he was seeing it again in all its glory he knew that Earth held far more than ever he had realized.

The miles pounded away under the bouncing wheels,

and slowly the agricultural vista gave way to the gaunt, stark industrial area that he remembered from his last brief visit to White Sands. There were acres of concrete, wide roads, army camps, factories, foundries and machine shops; there were gantries pointing their fingers to the sky, but there were not so many as he remembered from before. They were more widely spread, the gaps between them showed large and empty, and Benbow remembered when they had clustered the earth for mile upon mile as far as the astonished eye could see.

One every seven or eight days—that was all that White Sands could manage now; before it had been one a day.

They passed a convoy of fuel tankers, huge ten-wheeled vehicles, their drivers seated high in their cabs, each with an armed guard in the passenger seat.

"That right you come back from Mars?"

The question startled Benbow from his introspection, and he grinned as he realized that the wizened brown-faced driver had at last plucked up courage to speak to him.

"Yes, that's right. I left there—oh, must be seven months or more ago."

"I got a whisper from the office that there'd be a passenger this trip."

"News travels fast." Benbow wondered just how.

"Yeah. That guy at the space station—"

"Duclos?"

"The Frenchie, yeah. He radioed down."

Benbow nodded absently, and turned again to his inspection of the industrial complex through which they drove.

"What's it like there?" asked the driver.

"Mars? Oh, just like the desert here on Earth." How could you tell about it? And would he be believed if he told the truth?

"The Sahara, eh?"

"Yes, something like, only it's not hot. In fact, it gets damned cold at night." How did you explain it? How did you

109

talk about the unremiting battle against the cold, the sand, the lack of air and of water?

"Why'd you come back?"

And that was a hell of a question, too. Benbow had wondered about his reception; he had talked about it with Mueller before he left, and the old man had given him a letter which was quite noncommital. It gave Benbow all the voyage back to think up his own story for officialdom, and he had done it. What was meant for officialdom would hardly do for a semi-literate American truck driver.

"You won't believe me," he said seriously.

"Try me."

"Well, I came back to see a girl."

There was a moment's silence that was broken, at last, by a cackle of laugher from beside him.

"Hey, that must be some chick. All the way from Mars to see a chick. What is she? An angel or something?"

"Yes," said Benbow. "Yes, I guess you could say that."

The truck stopped at last in a wide concrete drive that led between broad green lawns up to the main entrance of a four-storied building. The two rocket men bade Benbow a brief farewell, and the wizened driver took him in through the main entrance of the building.

In the lobby it was cool and shadowed; the concrete floor was cool under his feet, and an air conditioning plant wafted an icy breeze that made him shiver after the heat outside. There was a long, wooden reception desk to the left and Benbow followed the driver across to it.

Two women, middle aged and in green uniform dresses, manned a small telephone exchange at the rear of the desk, and another, younger woman rose from the stool on which she was perched as they approached.

"Hallo, Hank. Good run?"

"Yeah, no trouble. I brought along your passenger."

The girl turned curious eyes on Benbow.

"The man from Mars. The whole base knows about you. You're the first one to come back."

Benbow smiled. "It's good to be home again."

The girl pursed her lips to a thin line, and Benbow noticed for the first time the lines of strain drawn deep in the flesh of her cheeks and at the corners of her eyes. They were the eyes of someone who had lived on a knife edge for far too long; they were the same sort of eyes that the driver had possessed, now that he thought about it, and the two men on the rocket.

The girl said tautly, "You don't know what you're saying, Mr. Benbow."

So, they knew his name. Duclos had been busy.

"Is it that bad?"

She ignored the question as if it was not worthy of an answer. "Go along the main corridor to the door at the end marked Private. The General is expecting you."

The General? Benbow smiled his thanks and walked away from the desk in the direction she pointed. His steps rang on the solid floor, and through open doors he could hear the clack of typewriters and the clatter of teleprinters. It was hard to realize that this cool, modern building with its air of calm efficiency was part of a collapsing empire that tottered on the brink of an eternal, bottomless abyss.

He knocked on the door and went through.

Behind the door an elderly man in faded blue denims rose from a table, replacing a phone on its cradle as he did so.

"Mr. Benbow." It was a statement not a question. "The General wants to see you at once. Through that door."

Benbow nodded and went through the gray door which the old man indicated. Beyond it was a large office made cool by venetian blinds drawn down to keep out the heat of the noonday sun. From a metal desk the figure of a man rose to greet him—a man with a black eye patch and a tin leg, a man with white hair that Benbow remembered had once been gray, a man who had been straight despite his physical afflictions, a man who was now bent and old long before his time. Only the one good eye remained as Benbow recalled it. It was bright and diamond hard, and

111

it looked at Benbow with a coldness that he had seen only in deep space.

"Why, General Kramer! You've been promoted since I was here last."

"Promotion! The trappings of a dying age, Mr. Benbow. I suppose I should know you. To my regret I have sent too many people to Mars. I remember none of them." The single eye fixed Benbow like an arrow. "Why have you come back?"

XIX

KRAMER SPAT out the question with a venom that was as alarming as it was disconcerting. Benbow felt a momentary bewilderment. He had expected curiosity, disbelief, perhaps even sarcasm; but Kramer's question exhibited none of these. There was a hostility in his tone of voice and his manner that Benbow couldn't understand. Kramer acted and sounded as if Benbow were an intruder, someone who had no right to be here, at White Sands. He wondered for a moment if Kramer were joking, but the idea was too ludicrous for long consideration. All these thoughts, and others, sped through his brain in the space of a second that was frozen and held as they stood and looked at each other—Kramer staring coldly with his one good eye, Benbow returning that stare with growing bewilderment.

"Perhaps if I sat down—" He said tentatively.

"All right. Sit down, sit down." Kramer resumed his own seat and the tin leg creaked as he reached down with both hands and folded it into place. "Now, I'll ask you again—why have you come back?"

The break had at least given Benbow time to marshal his thoughts. He decided that the cover story he had concocted during the trip was the one he would have to rely on. It was too late to improvise, and it was too early even to think about reaching Drusilla. He reached into his tunic and took out the letter that Mueller had given him. Silently, he handed it to Kramer who slit the envelope and read the brief contents.

He dropped it on the desk and waved a hand in vague dismissal. "This doesn't tell me anything, Benbow, except that you were here by permission, and with the help of Heinz Mueller. It doesn't tell me why."

"Professor Mueller felt that the reason would be better told by word of mouth," replied Benbow.

"Then tell me—by word of mouth." The sarcasm was clear.

"Mueller realizes that you have had little time to do more than marshal your resources to the task of maintaining this base and supplying the Mars Project. He has had no direct contact with the way things are going on Earth for a long time. Oh, yes," Benbow waved away Kramer's interruption, "we've had news of things from new arrivals and by radio direct from here, but there hasn't been any really concentrated effort to find out exactly how things are progressing."

"I can tell you that in one sentence," growled Kramer.

"Can you?" countered Benbow. "Mueller made a lot of predictions about what would happen. They were made a long time ago and he wants to know if there has been any radical departure from the line of progression that he laid down. If there has been—"

"How do you fit in?"

"I'm a biologist."

Kramer slouched in his chair, his one eye hooded and brooding. "So—the rumors have reached Mars." He spoke almost to himself. "I thought they would, eventually."

"What rumors?" Benbow knew that his voice was harsh and that the question was abrupt. It was drawn from him by something that was quite inexplicable, something bred within him by the General's reaction to his cover story, Kramer acted as if he was a spy. "What rumors?" he insisted.

For answer the General reached across his desk and punched a button on the intercom unit. "Get Salinger and Simon in here."

113

Benbow felt alarm growing inside him. What had he said that could arouse such a reaction? He had expected ridicule if he told the true reason for his return—and he had countered it as best he could. But, having done that, what was wrong? Kramer seemed almost to have expected him —or someone like him on just such a mission as he had described; his reactions were those of a man who was faced by something that he had anticipated.

And that was it!

Benbow realized with a shock that he was not only expected but his story was anticipated; and that was as crazy as the nightmare through which he had lived for so long. This was another facet of the never-ending torture of his life and times. And he was only one among millions.

The office door opened and two men came in. One of them was bulky and middle-aged, with a gray face and piercing black eyes set in deep hollow sockets. The other was a younger man, his complexion was sallow and unlined, his hair black and oiled, his shoulders stooped and crooked.

Kramer stabbed a finger at each of them in turn. The plump one was Salinger, the thin one was Simon; Benbow acknowledged each of them as they nodded to him.

"Mr. Benbow," said Kramer, "has, this day, arrived from Mars. It seems, gentlemen, that Mueller wants to know what is happening here on Earth."

"Don't you know?" asked Simon wryly.

"No, I don't."

"Can't you guess?" enquired Salinger. "You have heard something to bring you back here."

The charade was back with him again. Benbow said, "I know nothing, neither have I heard anything."

"These two officers," broke in Kramer, "are members of my personal staff. They will see that you have anything that you want in the way of facilities and information." He chuckled coldly. "Especially information. You can go anywhere you wish within the area under my control. One thing—" the single eye fixed him with an almost malevolent glare—"any report you wish to make will be seen by me first. Is that clear?"

Benbow licked his lips, afraid of what he might say. He nodded dumbly.

"Then that's all." Kramer nodded and turned his head to a file of papers. Clearly, the interview was at an end.

Outside in the brilliant afternoon sun Benbow paused to gather himself with a conscious effort. He was more disturbed by Kramer's attitude than he would have thought possible. Earth was in turmoil, but that wasn't new; there was martial control of the White Sands base, and that wasn't new either. He had come to Earth to find Drusilla; suddenly, that didn't seem so important. Africa was far away now, much farther away than it had been when he was on Mars, and there was a very large question mark written clearly before him.

Suddenly, coming home was something to worry about.

Hank, the driver, was waiting for him in the shade of a large tree that grew close to the concrete drive, and he waved a greasy hand to attract Benbow's attention.

"Got orders to take you to your quarters, Mr. Benbow."

"Well, thanks." Benbow smiled. "I'm glad someone is friendly around here."

"The General give you a hard time?"

"You could say that."

"Hard man, that Kramer." He gunned the car towards the main entrance. "Had a pal of mine shot last month for looting an empty house." He turned on to the main road and changed gear. "Still, I guess discipline is important—after all, we've been warned about looting."

Benbow felt dismay that official murder could be so lightly dismissed. He remembered the salvoes that he had heard in Buxton; he thought about Quince and his sad bloodhound face. Quince, with the weight of the world on his conscience, laughing when he heard of the revolt which surely meant his death.

From the distance, and above the noise of the car engine, came a booming roar that grew and mounted. Hank pulled the car off the roadway and switched off the motor. He pointed away to the left between two buildings, and said, "Just there, Mr. Benbow. Look just about there."

Benbow looked in the direction pointed out by the greasy forefinger, and he saw a flash of light low down on the horizon. It was a light that grew and lifted into the heavens, leaving behind it a pillar of white cloud that boiled and billowed outwards from some central point. He had to shade his eyes against the sunlight, but he could see it quite clearly now, the silver pencil that gleamed small as it lifted itself clear of the planet that had given it birth.

"The first one in more than a week," said the driver softly. "Still, I guess while we're doing that, we're living." He switched on the engine and they went on their way.

The car took Benbow to a large, barrack-like hostel where a motherly middle-aged Negress took charge of him and allocated him a small, cramped cubicle with a bed, a chair and a small cupboard. The furnishings were cold and meager, but at least he was alone, and that was different from Mars. His belongings were few enough and they were quickly stowed in the cupboard.

Benbow sat down on the edge of the hard cot and wondered what he should do. It was mid-afternoon—his first day back on Earth—and he felt lost, alone, a stranger on an alien planet. All those long weeks and months on Mars had left their mark, and he knew that the scar was deeper than he would have thought possible. He had thought that there would be joy in coming home, in knowing that he was that much nearer to Drusilla. Now, he knew, distance was relative, and she was farther from him now than she had ever been before.

A quiet knock at the door disturbed him, but before he could call out the door opened and the lean, stooped figure of Simon stepped inside.

"Settling in all right?"

Benbow realized that the question was rhetorical, an opening gambit that didn't call for an answer. He nodded, and Simon was satisfied. The excuse had gained him entrance; its purpose was served. He pulled up a chair close beside the cot and sat across it straddle-legged, with his arms folded along the back.

"You're English?"

Again, Benbow nodded.

"How well do you know Mueller?"

"Now that's a hell of a question!" Benbow knew that his amazement showed.

"You must have been trusted for him to send you back here to find out what was going on." The sallow face was almost hawk-like. "And if he trusted you why did his letter of introduction give you no explicit mandate?"

"I've already explained that to Kramer." Benbow rose from the cot angrily. "Dammit, Simon, what the hell does it matter? I was the one who came back. It's as simple as that."

"If you wanted to know so much why didn't you ask by radio?" snapped Simon. "Didn't you trust us to give you a straight answer? Is that it?"

"Of course not." Benbow said wearily. "Look, Kramer let me know pretty clearly that he would censor anything I sent back. I don't need it spelled out for me, Simon. He doesn't even have to let me submit a report if he doesn't want to. He can make the reports in my name and no one will be any the wiser."

Simon glowered at him suspiciously.

"What are you trying to hide?" insisted Benbow. "Am I some sort of spy?"

"You could be."

"Then would I tell Kramer the reason why I came back? It doesn't make sense."

Simon studied him intently for several long seconds. "No," he shook his head, "it doesn't, and that's why you're being given free reign. If you are a spy then you're the stupidest, most innocent—" He shook his head in sudden disgust, and stood up pushing the chair from him. "Was it the rumors that brought you back?"

Benbow spread his arms wide in a gesture of sheer desperation.

"Rumors! That's what Kramer asked." He shook his head. "Simon, I don't know what the hell you're talking about. But one thing I have learned in my few hours here."

"And that is?"

"Kramer is scared stiff that Mueller knows something—or suspects something that Kramer doesn't want him to know."

Simon eyed him stonily for a long moment. Then he said, "Don't think too much, Benbow, it may destroy the illusion of your innocence."

The door slammed behind him as he left.

XX

LATER, IN THE relative cool of the evening, Benbow went down to the mess hall for a meal. It was unsatisfactory from all points of view. The food was mush, the bread stale, but the coffee was good. The main trouble lay within himself—and he knew it.

He had lain on his hard cot for a long time after Simon left him; he had thought and worried, and it had done no good. The worry continued as he ate his slop, but gradually it was driven from him by the stress of other things.

The news of his arrival had spread like wildfire, and he came to realize that, as the first person to return from Mars, he was something unique. Everyone wanted to ask him questions about Mars; they sought him out for reassurance, though he didn't realize it at first. They wanted to ask about friends who had left Earth months or years before; and they were curious that Benbow didn't know everyone there. There was an overpowering belief that Mars was like a small village, a closed community where everyone knew everybody. It was incomprehensible to them that Benbow didn't know more than a few score of the Martian community. They expected him to be on first name terms with everyone who'd ever gone there.

He talked for almost two hours with a large group that was continually changing, as men and women came to eat, and then left to work or to sleep. His own body cried out for rest, but he was kept talking, answering questions.

And, at last, he began to realize why!

He was the one man who could tell them what they wanted to know. He was the living proof that all they were doing and all they were sacrificing was not in vain. There was a sense of wonder that grew slowly within him as they came and talked and went away happier than when they came, their backs a little straighter, their eyes a little brighter.

To begin with Benbow was happy; true, he was tired, but the thought that he was bringing some sort of purpose to his ever-changing audience gave him the strength to carry on. They were drawing their purpose and their goal

118

from him, and while he had the strength he would help them.

And then he thought of the two great ships building on Diemos!

What was the old saying about being a prophet in your own land?

The weariness came back even more strongly. Now, he was talking in half truths, keeping back a major factor that he couldn't reveal. The strength slipped from him, and he broke away at last, dead tired, unhappy, longing only for the peace and oblivion of sleep. Back in his tiny cubicle the air was stale and heavy; sleep would not come. Benbow tossed and turned on the hard cot and sweated in the unaccustomed humidity, his nerves taut like bow strings as sleep refused to comfort him.

Simon woke him soon after dawn.

Benbow had a headache and his mouth was stale and sticky; his eyes were gummed and the stubble on his face was more difficult to remove than usual. Breakfast in the mess hall was as unappetizing as had been his meal of the evening before, and while he ate it Simon made small talk that was all too clearly designed to conceal the real puspose of his early visit.

Sheer bad temper prevented Benbow from being drawn into the questions which he wanted to ask, and his temper was not improved by the sardonic glances of amusement that Simon favored him with from time to time. Both of them played out the game to its finale.

It was a finale that began in the open seats of a scout car, and ended as the car drove on to the tarmac of an airstrip. A large jet stood gleaming in the early morning sun, the ground crew still working on it as the car pulled alongside.

Simon waved a hand towards the black mouth of the entry hatch.

"In there is the answer to all those questions you wanted to ask. You wanted knowledge, Benbow. Well, there it is—your doorway to wisdom. I hope you find what you want."

Benbow followed him up the ramp and into the cool interior of the plane. As he stepped on to the main deck the bulky form of Salinger came to greet him.

119

"Both of Kramer's aides." Benbow commented ironically. "I am honored, indeed."

"You may be now—you may not be soon," replied Salinger. "Come on up to the main cabin. We take off in ten minutes."

From the air, as they lifted from the tarmac, White Sands looked peaceful. A large industrial town basking in the sun under a summer sky. They lifted high into the heavens, heading northeast, and Benbow's curiosity grew by the moment.

After a while Salinger went up to the flight deck and Simon sat down beside Benbow. The great jets were only a murmur in the pressurized cabin, and they provided a back cloth to Simon's quiet voice as he asked, "Now, Benbow. The truth. Why did you come back?"

"I already told you," said Benbow bitterly.

"You want to find out how things are going. All right," Simon nodded, "I'll accept that for the moment. Let's go a step further. Why do you want to know?"

"Look," said Benbow shifting awkwardly in his seat, "we've been all over this—"

"And you still maintain that you weren't sent back because of the rumors that have reached Mars?" insisted Simon.

Benbow didn't even bother to answer.

"We can't believe," Simon went on, "that anyone would be so stupid as to stick his head in the lion's mouth without making some effort to protect himself. Because of that we're giving you the benefit of the doubt—"

"Well, thank you."

"We're prepared to believe your ignorance."

Benbow said icily, "Then perhaps you can tell me what this charade is all about."

"We can show you rather than tell," replied Simon. "What we can show you will prepare you for what we shall tell you. Maybe you'll believe us—maybe you won't. Either way it won't make a great deal of difference."

They flew on in silence. Benbow sat with his face turned to the window. There was nothing to see except sky and cloud. The ground was too far below for any detail to be seen clearly, and after a while he dozed, thankful that he could do so.

He was awakened by Simon who shook his arm and dragged him back from the abyss with a start of fear that twisted his stomach and jerked him to full wakefulness.

"We're heading down," said Simon. "Soon you'll be able to see what we have brought you to see."

"Where are we?" asked Benbow.

"The eastern seaboard of the former United States."

Benbow relaxed and turned towards the window. The jet noise was deeper, a thrumming sound that boomed through the cabin more certainly than the higher note of greater speed.

The clouds broke beneath them, and they entered a world that was gray and rainswept. Heavy squalls cast patterns in the air for miles around the speeding jet. Here one could see for a great distance; but there the rain limited visibility to little more than a mile. And the ground came slowly up to meet them as the jet slid along its shallow glide path.

There were wide areas of country spread below them, a vast panorama that was wet and misted, with rain that drowned it in heavy, semi-tropical storms. Their speed had dropped considerably, and Benbow judged that they were now flying at a little under a thousand feet. From this height there were broken houses to be seen, ruined towns and villages, roads that were set and deserted. The massive stretch of a continental highway swept beneath them, its lanes empty, it bridges wrecked and crumbling from ill treatment and lack of maintenance, a wide, shining, black ribbon that once had born the traffic of a booming civilization. The entire scene had an air of utter abandonment that was depressing.

After a long time Benbow asked, "How far are we from the coast?"

Simon chuckled. "I wondered if you had lost your tongue."

"There's not a great deal to get enthusiastic over. How far?"

"A little over fifty miles."

Fifty miles! Benbow felt the questions rising like a tide within him, born on a wave of excitement that mounted as realization came to him.

"But—" he hesitated, uncertain how to go on. "But, the mists! Surely we wouldn't see the ground from this height?"

Simon said nothing.

Benbow hardly noticed his silence, because the questions were piling up in his mind as his eyes sought eagerly for the details of a landscape that should have been blotted from his sight by the evil, too-well remembered miasma of the Weed. All that he could see was wet and rainswept; the lowering clouds clutched wispy tentacles at the plane, but they were insubstantial, they lacked the heavy, boiling consistency of the Weed-born coverlet he had known in Africa and Britain.

Ahead he could see the coast line, a bleak and broken edge of earth that looked as if it had been cut off jaggedly by some gigantic plough. The ground here was bare and black, with naked rocks and fantastic, jumbled outcroppings where some huge force had tilted the whole landscape, scouring the soil and all that grew upon it, burning and destroying in a holocaust of fury and destruction.

This must be the edge of the earthquake that he had heard about on Mars. This was where the eastern seaboard had shivered and groaned, and slid slowly under the Atlantic ocean.

His eyes refused to believe what they saw as the coast line swept beneath them. From this height he could see clearly all around him a gray and desolate waste, but—harsh though it was—it wasn't what he had expected to see. This was no mist-covered, Weed-tangled ocean. This was the Atlantic in all its former fury, with waves lashing high on a mountainous sea that boiled and bubbled; creamed waves reached fingers high into the air, and the heavens poured down more water upon the water below.

He felt stunned and shaken, at once appalled and excited; there was within him a jumble of emotion that outstripped anything that he had ever known before in the whole of his tortuous, tormented life.

The jet backed away to the right, turning at right angles to its previous course.

"Look there," Simon called, and his hand came over Benbow's shoulder pointing out towards the east. "Benbow, look there."

And, as he looked, Benbow could see the cloud lowering itself from the heavens to join up with the sea beneath. Not two miles from where they flew the mists that he remembered so well built a solid wall from sea to sky. Here, the seas were not so tempestuous, the waves were smaller and the surface had an oily, unclean texture; large islands floated and tossed, and, as he looked, Benbow saw that one of them was split scross the middle so that a channel was forming which would divide it, shortly, in two pieces. The glimpse was a momentary one and then the speeding jet had left it far behind. But it was enough—it told Benbow all that he needed to know, it answered all questions that rang within his stunned, confused brain.

He turned his wondering gaze back to Simon who sat quiet beside him, unmoved and unmoving.

"The Weed, Simon," he said wonderingly, "it—it's going."

XXI

SIMON NODDED. "Dying is the word."

"How—how long has this been going on?"

"It started just over a year ago. Once the volcanic action began the Weed stopped spreading. The earthquake here broke its hold on the land, and once the ocean swept in with its reborn storms and waves, well," he shrugged, "the Weed never regained its grip."

The jet banked again and turned back toward the coast. From the forward cabin the bulky form of Salinger appeared. His gray face was creased in a smile that had no humor in it, and the black eyes seemed even more deeply set because of the lines etched in the cheeks by the twisted grin.

"Have you learned enough, Benbow?" he asked.

"Enough?" Benbow felt the elation growing within him. "Don't you realize what this will mean, Salinger?"

"We've known for almost a year. You think we haven't thought about it?" Salinger slumped his heavy form into the seat on the other side of the gangway. "You think we've been sitting on our backsides wondering what we should do about it? Isn't that why you came back from Mars—to see what

123

we have shown you? And now that you have seen it, Benbow—what now?"

Behind the elation Benbow felt a growing anxiety as Salinger pounded the questions at him. Each of them had an answer, and each answer was frightening in its implications.

"You think we haven't thought about it?" Of course they'd thought about it, they must have done. It meant that the World was throwing off the shackles; it meant that Man could start the long climb back. With the Mars base to back them up—

"You think we've been sitting on our backsides wondering what we should do about it?" They shouldn't have needed to think; the course of action was clear before them and yet they hadn't done anything. Mars still didn't know what was happening!

"Is—is it like this all over?"

Salinger nodded. "The Pacific is in even better shape. A string of volcanoes was thrown up from the ocean bed, and they cleared thousands of square miles. The mists are worse there because the Weed is dying from the center outwards. The seas off the China coast are clear, but the Mediterranean is a shambles. The Weed is almost gone, but what it has left behind isn't very pretty."

"Tell me," said Benbow.

"The lower half of Italy is below the sea, Greece is drowned, and the western half of Turkey. Gibraltar has gone and southern Spain along with it. The entire north African coastline is a deserted waste right through to the Nile Valley." He looked away from Benbow. "We still don't know about Great Britain. The Weed hasn't cleared from there and the mists still cover the whole of western Europe. Not too many people get out from there these days. In fact, I don't think we've had one for almost six months. News is hard to come by all round. All we learn is what we get from scouting trips by planes such as this.

"All we really know—or care about—is that the Weed is going, and going fast."

Benbow didn't need a map drawn for him. Salinger had painted a clear picture in crisp sentences that drew a general outline into which he could fill the details. And it was the detail that was important.

A lot was guesswork, speculation, but there was enough to tell him that here—stark and clear—was the missing factor that he had tried so hard to find while he was on Mars. This was the one thing that Mueller had not foreseen. No one could possibly have foreseen it because the facts were not there. They were hidden by the X factor that he had seen but dimly, but which was now crystallised and translated before him.

The entire planet had changed these past horrible years; the weather, the temperature, the entire ecology of the world had been disrupted by something which had created its own conditions. And in those conditions had lain the seed of its own destruction. The Weed had grown and flourished and spread, but that had been in the days before the increase of ultraviolet from the Sun, before the mists and the humidity, before the rise in temperature had melted the ice caps, before the quakes and the tremors and the volcanoes.

Now, the Weed was dying.

True, the quakes and the volcanoes would go on. There would be years of struggle and disappointment, decades before things began to revert to normal. A century perhaps. But the first crack had appeared in the wall of chaos, and it would grow larger with the passing of the years until the seas were clear and the skies were mist free.

The Weed was dying.

Benbow wondered if he should have foreseen it? Could anyone have foreseen it? Mueller, perhaps, or Svenson? He doubted it. Some things could be deduced with a cold, clear logic; but coldness and clarity were not the things that the Weed fostered. There had been an urgency and a despair in everything that Man had done; Mueller had pointed the way into the future and Man had gone along that way because it was the only road open to him—the only road that led anywhere. Mueller had been a man in a million—yet he had not foreseen this.

There was still so much that was unanswered. Simon had said that they had known about it for almost a year. That was five months before Benbow left Mars, and yet no word had filtered through.

He thought about it; he thought about Kramer's suspicious welcome; about Simon and Salinger.

Below him the coast line sped and fell behind; the wild, bleak country of the seaboard was gaunt and terrible under torrential rain squalls. Beyond it the land was green and lush; there was no mist to cover it; there was no sun to draw the mist from the ground. And this was the important factor. Once the Weed had gone the mists would vanish from the seas, the meteorological conditions would revert; there would be rainstorms such as the World had never seen since the days of prehistory, but the rain would wash the skies clean of mist and sulphur, the clouds would break eventually and the sun would regain its true position. There would be wind and weather, cold as well as heat, the humidity would fall, the ice caps would return to the poles, and the sea would give up those lands which it had swamped. Mankind could begin the long, hard climb back.

It would take centuries, but even within his lifetime, Benbow knew, things would start to improve. They could bring back from Mars the technicians and the experts that would be needed; the flow of knowledge and materials would be reversed, and over the millions of miles of space the Mars base could succour the world that had given it birth.

If they knew about it!

"Why hasn't Mars been told?" he asked the question simply yet there was a stark demand born by his voice that robbed it of that simplicity.

Simon looked away from him, evasion written on every muscle of his lean, olive face. From Salinger there was only tight lipped grimness.

"Well?"

"Kramer forbade it." Salinger spoke softly, hardly audibly as he condemned by his tone of voice the decision of his superior.

Benbow felt his bewilderment growing. "Why? In God's name—why?"

"White Sands is the last organized base of civilization in the world—as far as we know," Salinger told him.

"That has no bearing—"

"It has every bearing," rasped Salinger. "Benbow, you've seen what is happening. You know what it means. It means that the tide is turning and we can start rebuilding."

"That's too obvious—"

"It means something else," Salinger told him grimly. "It means that White Sands is growing in power. Every week saw control of the central area of the American continent growing and spreading. Already, we've turned our backs on the precipice and we're heading back up the mountain. Every month sees another town or another village or another city brought under our control. Another area adds its quota to our power and our rebirth. Benbow, White Sands is far stronger now than it was three years ago."

Benbow digested the information. He had no reason to doubt Salinger, indeed, under the circumstances, it was the only logical thing that could happen.

"I still don't see—"

"Kramer is the military dictator of the whole area," Simon said wearily. "His word is law, his decisions are final. We are controlled by one man, Benbow, and that is a situation that leaves a great deal to be desired."

"There is still Mueller," said Benbow. "He has a measure of control."

"And there you have it," snapped Salinger. "Kramer believes that Mars is sapping the lifeblood of Earth. He believes that Mueller is building his own empire at the expense of the home planet. If we're getting stronger, why do you think the rockets are leaving less frequently? Oh, I know," he waved away Benbow's interruption, "you thought Earth was falling down, slipping away. You thought we were heading for the same fate as Woomera. Well, we weren't."

"Kramer is stockpiling his resourcees," put in Simon, "against the day when he can send an expedition to take over control of the Martian base."

"He's mad!"

"A megalomaniac, perhaps. But mad?" Salinger shook his head. "He thinks that Mueller will want to abandon the Mars base when he knows what is happening here. He believes that all the people on Mars will start flooding back as quickly as they can, and he doesn't want that."

"Dammit, why?"

"He wants the base maintained, he wants to stay in space and develop our control of the planets. He thinks that we have a chance to do two things—to rebuild Earth and to conquer the Solar System. To do that he has to have control of the Mars base."

Benbow laughed weakly, hysteria bubbling within him.

"There's another reason," said Simon coldly. "All we know about Mars is how strong is our base there, how it is growing in size, how the people are building tall and strong and vigorously on the backs of the people here, on Earth. Kramer wants control of that power so that he can use it for his own ends, and he fears that if Mueller is warned then he will have no opportunity of displacing Mueller by his own authority. If Kramer can control Mars he doubles the size of his empire."

The hysteria grew inside Benbow, jerking the muscles of his throat and stomach. He thought of the dingy shanty town that nestled feebly under the futile plastic of the domes; he thought of the shabby huts, the hard, never-ending work, the rations, the sterilized air, the longing for Earth. He thought of Martha Dresden and her Mars-born children, of Mueller and Svenson and their wild, impossible dreams, of Larson and his eternal spirituals.

This was the tall, strong, vigorous empire that Simon had spoken about and Kramer believed in; this huddled shambles of a displaced persons' camp resting timidly on the red, alien sands of a planet that could swallow them in an instant. And Kramer wanted it to waste the strength of a reborn Earth.

"If you could see it." There were tears in Benbow's eyes, tears of pain as well as hysteria. "If you could only see it."

"We only know what you tell us," said Salinger quietly. "All we know are the pictures painted over the radio by Mueller and his people in their reports."

"What do you expect?" rasped Benbow. "A true picture? One to destroy the morale of White Sands and its people? Do you want us to tell you how we struggle to survive, how we make do with skimpy, jerrybuilt huts under plastic domes? Do you want to know about the sand storms, the cold, the lack of air? Do we have to advertise the strain of living on a knife edge from day to day? Do we need to destroy your will to survive by telling you the truth?"

There was a long silence. The note of the engines was higher now, but within the cabin the silence seemed so finely drawn that Benbow could hear his heart pounding within him. Simon was looking out of the window, and Salinger looked at the floor with eyes that were blacker and deeper than ever, his face gray and dead.

"We only know what you have told us," Simon insisted softly. "And Kramer believes it."

The passion and the hysteria drained from Benbow. He felt weak and helpless as he asked, "Just what does he want?"

"Control of the Mars base with Mueller subject to his orders and his control."

"Under these conditions?" Benbow was incredulous. "What does Earth mean to him? Can't he see that Mars doesn't matter a damn?"

Salinger shrugged. "He thinks that he can do everything that needs to be done here, and maintain the Mars base. He believes that, with the base to supply the technicians, Earth can be rebuilt and Mars maintained—and he wants full control."

"Mueller will give it to him," said Benbow coldly.

"Will he?" asked Simon. "Are you sure? Mueller was put in sole charge by the combined governments of an Earth that is dead and gone forever. Can you give up that authority for him?"

Benbow looked numbly at the two men. Simon was right. How could he speak for Mueller? How could he know what Mueller might do when confronted by a dictatorial demand from a military dictator.

Wearily, Simon said, "We'll be landing soon."

XXII

IT WAS NOON, and the sun was high and hot, the air humid and heavy. To Benbow, as they landed, the day seemed dark and shadowed despite the brightness.

129

As they left the plane, he said, "Aren't you afraid of what I might say to people?"

"What can you say?" countered Salinger. "You're not really in a position to stir up trouble, are you?"

"Why have you told me all this?"

"Kramer ordered it. He wanted to know if you were really the spy he thought you were." Salinger grinned crookedly. "He thought your reactions would give you away, and I think we can safely report to him that you were as surprised as you ought to be."

If only they knew, thought Benbow. He giggled inanely as he remembered the two ships on Diemos. In five or six months Mars base would be only a shell manned by a few hundred people—Mueller among them. How much of a conquest would that be for Kramer? The laughter bubbled within him and he saw the grim alarm on the faces of Simon and Salinger.

And then the laughter died. Benbow shivered despite the noonday heat as a cold sweat trembled through him. With the Mars base denuded what aid could there be for the reviving corpse of Earth? What help would there be from the thousands of experts and technicians and scientists heading out of the Solar System for a new life and a new beginning—if they found that which they sought.

"Are you all right, Benbow?"

He met the worried eyes of Salinger and managed a feeble, unhysterical grin. "Do you expect me to be after the past few hours?"

"Kramer will want to see you later on—after we've made our joint report."

"Salinger," said Benbow, "do you really believe that Kramer is right? Do you really think that we can split our resources like this and get away with it?"

The plump man shrugged. "How do I know? Kramer is a leader of men—of that there is no doubt. How do I know whether or not he can do it?"

"We're dependent upon each other," Benbow told him. "Mars is doomed without aid from Earth. Earth could be doomed if we try to do too much." He brooded for a second, and said, "If Kramer and Mueller could get together—"

"It would mean that one has to convince the other what is the correct course," broke in Salinger, "and I can't see Kramer giving an inch."

"But if the ultimate good of Earth is involved—"

"It's been a long morning." Salinger put a hand on Benbows shoulder. "Let's eat."

Lunch was eaten in silence in a corner of the mess hall. The food was better than his two previous meals; there was cold meat and salad, the bread was new and dark brown, and there was a white, sweet cheese to go with it. The hall was crowded and Benbow sat next to the wall. He noticed how Simon and Salinger gently dissuaded people from questioning him as they had done the day before. For that he wasn't sorry; he had a lot to think about.

One thing was clear—though, so far, it had not been mentioned—Kramer would have to achieve a military take-over of the Mars base. It was the only sort of control he was likely to achieve. It meant that Kramer was hording his resources—stockpiling, Simon had said—as White Sands grew in power and authority. It meant that no uncensored news was allowed to reach Mars from Earth, and that was why any report he wished to make to Mueller had to be vetoed by Kramer.

It was utterly crazy, Benbow told himself. The situation bore within it the final dissolution of civilization because Kramer's bid for power was bound to fail. The time element was against Kramer although he didn't realize it. Even if it was sent tomorrow any force destined for Mars would not get there until after the two ships had left Diemos; and if that happened then Kramer would not only fail on Mars, he would fail on Earth as well.

The final piece of dark bread was dry in his mouth, the hunger in his stomach was gone, but it had been banished by other things than food.

Abruptly, he asked, "When can I see Kramer?"

He saw Simon and Salinger exchange a rapid glance.

"Why the hurry?" asked Simon.

"Because I know a great deal more than Kramer knows," said Benbow. "And I want to tell him the real reason I came back to Earth." He smiled wistfully. "Though I doubt

131

if he will believe me any more than he believed what I told him before."

"You sound too smug," Salinger commented. "You've thought about this, you've seen what there is to see. You should be scared, frightened by the implications," his black eyes were hooded by suspicion, "and yet you're not. You're too smug and self satisfied. What do you know, Benbow?"

Benbow turned in his seat and looked the man full in the face. "Oh, I'm scared, Salinger. I've been scared for a long time, for most of my life I've been frightened of one thing or another. I'm like you—and you as well, Simon—I've lived with fear too long for one more episode to make its mark. As I said, I know more than Kramer. I have a fact at my disposal that he does not, and it is something that makes nonsense of his threat to the Mars base. That is why I want to see him as soon as possible."

Simon drained his coffee and set the cup on the table. "What about now?" He grinned lopsidedly. "I'm curious, Salinger."

Salinger lifted his bulk clear of the table, and Benbow could read the puzzlement in his eyes. Salinger was typical of the vast majority of people today, both on Earth and on Mars. They had only their own individual pictures born of imagination and created by distrust. He could not blame any of them.

On Mars, Mueller's people distrusted the ability of Earth to survive and recover; the distrust was created because they had no true information of the situation. On Earth, Kramer had a false picture of Mars and the base, a picture created by Mueller because he saw the need to keep up the morale at White Sands.

"Well?" said Salinger. "I thought you wanted to see Kramer?"

Benbow rose and followed them from the mess hall.

The car which had brought them from the airfield was still waiting, its driver dozing in the shade of a tree. It was two miles to Kramer's headquarters, and Benbow was glad that he didn't have to walk there after his lunch. He had a full belly and a feeling of well-being that was engendered as much by the thoughts and plans he had made as by the food he had eaten.

For the first time in a long while he was able to think of Drusilla without that background of fear that had dogged him for as long as he could remember. There was a confidence within him that had no basis in fact; he knew it to be ridiculous, yet he could do nothing to deny it. Drusilla was with O'Brien and he would have her with him soon.

Quince had said, "I will send her to you when I can," and that had been so long ago. Quince had been unable to fulfill that promise, but now—if she lived—Drusilla was within his reach once again. That was all that mattered.

Inside the large white cube of the building they went straight to Kramer's office. No one stopped them, although Benbow noticed that the guards and the receptionists on the front desk took careful note of their arrival.

Salinger led the way into the office without bothering to knock; Benbow supposed that it was some indication of his stature that he could do so. The white head of Kramer was turned away from them, his chair turned so that he could look out of the window.

"That you, Joe?" The voice was as harsh as Benbow remembered it from previous experience. He wondered if it ever softened.

"Yes, sir," said Salinger. "We just got back."

The chair swung round and the one good eye stabbed balefully at Benbow.

"You just got back. Well, Benbow, and what have you to tell us now?"

Benbow smiled slightly. "The real reason why I came back to Earth," he said it calmly, and felt more at peace than he had for a long time.

"Ah, the substance rather than the illusion. Sit down—tell me in comfort." Kramer nodded to a chair.

Benbow sat down and noticed that Simon stood close behind him while Salinger leaned against the wall beside a window, so that the sun cast his shadow across the carpeted floor.

"The real reason, Benbow," said Kramer softly. "No more prevarication, no more stories, no more pretence."

"None," agreed Benbow equably, "though I doubt that you will believe me now any more than you did before."

133

"I'll be the judge of that." The black patch over the missing eye was like a second, gaping mouth.

"I came back to find my wife."

No one moved. Salinger didn't even look away from the window. Simon was a statue out of his sight; Kramer an obelisk with one frozen eye set in a chalky face under white, sculpted hair.

"You ask us to believe that you are mad?" Kramer whispered.

"No, I ask you to believe that I am sane—the sanest man who ever lived because I found what I wanted before it was too late. I should never have left her to bear my child alone."

The chair creaked as Benbow relaxed. Now, it was told.

Kramer chuckled slightly, a chuckle that grew and mounted into a gust of ironic laughter that shook the room and accentuated the silence that had gone before. It echoed and billowed around Benbow, but he paid it no heed for he had expected it—that or something like it.

"You really expect us to believe that you left the safety of your Martian heaven to come back here, to this hell planet, for a woman?" Kramer leaned forward in his chair and rested his hands on the desk top. "Benbow, you are trying my patience too far."

Benbow shrugged. "I have seen what you wanted me to see, Kramer, and I am able to relate what I have seen to the position as I know it to be on Mars. I know both sides, I know things which you do not, things which affect every plan and every idea you have ever had about the relationship between Earth and the Mars base."

Kramer said nothing.

"When I tell you the full reason for my decision to return to Earth you will realize that what I have told you is true."

"Then surprise us once again," snapped Kramer.

Benbow shook his head. "Not yet, General, not yet. I want to bargain with you. The additional knowledge that I have is my main bargaining point."

"You're in no position to bargain."

"I think I am."

"If you have knowledge it is your duty to pass it on."

134

Benbow laughed outright. "Don't be pompous, Kramer, it makes you ridiculous."

"We can soon force it from you."

"Torture? Drugs? Perhaps you can. On the other hand you might lose valuable time, You might kill me, and that would rob you of an invaluable expert—although I say so —and you still wouldn't know what had died with me."

"At least we can hear what he wants, General." Salinger moved away from the window.

Kramer nodded slowly. "At least we can do that, Joe."

"What is it you want, Benbow?" asked Salinger.

"Bring my wife and child to me—here, at White Sands."

A game of chess played without queens. The thought was in Benbow's mind as he watched Kramer and waited for his reaction.

"You are not a stupid man." The single eye burned at him, at once icy and aflame. "Yet that request has the hallmark of stupidity."

"I know where they may be found. If I am right then she can be brought to me within a very short time. If she is not there, if she is—dead—" The thought choked in his throat. "Well, then that is the end of it."

Benbow rose stiffly from the chair and crossed to the window to stand beside Salinger. He felt hot and tired; there was no expectation in waiting for Kramer to say yes or no. All at once nothing mattered; he had come to the end of something that had started long ago, and now all he could do was stand aside and watch the final scene play itself out.

Kramer said nothing.

"There is a town called Butere north of Lake Victoria," said Benbow. "The maps will give the exact location. Close by is—or rather was—the home of a man named O'Brien. He knew the country and the tribesmen, and he was well thought of in the days before the Weed. She would go there if she could. One of your planes could make it there and back in a few hours."

"You can't land a jet in the middle of Africa," broke in Simon, "not without an airstrip."

"I know. There is an airstrip—"

"After all these years? Hell, it probably hasn't been used in the past decade."

"O'Brien was going to keep it clear if he could. Just in case."

"You're crazy," said Simon.

"It might be done," mused Salinger. "One of the small jets with a low landing speed. If the strip is smooth enough."

"Joe, you're as crazy as he is," snapped Simon.

And still Kramer held his peace.

"I had a wife once." Salinger moved away from the window and from Benbow. "I never had a chance to go back to her, and she never had a chance to come to me."

"If you'll go along," said Benbow, "I'll take your word for what you find there."

"Don't you want to go yourself?" asked Simon bitterly.

Benbow chuckled drily. "Do you think the General would allow that? I'm his hostage. If I know anything, Simon, then he has to safeguard it. Isn't that right, Kramer?"

"You're taking the decision out of my hands, Benbow," said Kramer. "You've convinced Salinger, but you haven't convinced me. Do you think I'm justified in risking men and planes to look for a woman and child who may very well be dead?"

"Do you think I care about justification?" retorted Benbow. "I came all this way back with one purpose in mind. I have come too far to give up easily. I know that I'm asking a great deal, but I have a great deal to offer in return—far more than you can ever guess."

"It would be an easy way out, General," said Salinger. "The whole thing will be over in a couple of days."

Kramer swung his chair round and turned his back on the three men. "All right, all right. But on one condition. Joe, if the airfield looks bad you turn straight round without even trying to make a landing."

"I'm not looking for trouble, General."

Kramer grunted. "Sir Galahad with a tin leg and a black eye patch. Get the hell out of here."

XXIII

SALINGER LEFT that night.

He calculated the difference in time between White Sands and Butere, and decided that there was no point in waiting. The plane was a converted scout jet with a cruising speed of fifteen hundred miles an hour.

"I reckon about six hours each way," he told Benbow. "If we take off around eight tonight we'll make a landing about ten in the morning local time at Butere. That'll give us plenty of time and daylight to look around." He eyed Benbow grimly. "I'm not hanging around, Benbow. I can't risk the plane or the crew. If we don't find anything before dusk—well, I'm heading out."

Benbow nodded. There was a limit to what he could ask of Salinger, and he knew all too well the feral fear of darkness which had been reborn in the minds of men over the past decade. It was the primal fear of the jungle where night creatures prowled, and where death in a thousand terrible forms was covered by the black night sky.

He didn't watch the take-off. There was no point. The airfield was a long way from his small, bare cubicle, and the evening was dark and humid. In the mess hall he ate a meal that made no impression either on his mind or his stomach, and later he lay down on his hard cot to sleep.

That sleep came rapidly was not surprising. Physically he was exhausted by the long day; mentally he was drained by what he had seen and by what he had been forced to do. The facts and facets of the past hours were jumbled within his brain in an overwhelming burden that seemed to drain all energy from him. There was a mounting tide to the events that had an element of chaos about it; he seemed borne on a wave that rushed with increasing fury upon an alien shore, yet he himself seemed aloof, suspended on the crest of that wave between heaven and earth as he was carried to the final catastrophe.

For the first time in many long months his sleep was disturbed by dreams of Drusilla, and they were dreams which turned to nightmares. He lay and groaned and sweated in the heavy atmosphere of his tiny room, and he didn't wake until the sun was high in the sky. He washed in dirty, brownish water to refresh himself, and by the time he got to the mess hall it was well after nine o'clock.

Salinger had been gone for thirteen hours.

There was an unbearable tension building within him that he had never know before. Over the years he had buried his feelings so many times that the scar tissue was thin and easily broken now. He held a raw and gaping wound that grew larger as the hours passed. Time dragged on leaden feet that moved so slowly that they seemed not to move at all, and Benbow suffered alternate bursts of excitement and optimism, fear and depression.

Salinger could be on his way back now.

He spent the morning walking aimlessly along concrete paths under the hot sun, afraid to move far from his room or from Kramer's headquarters, yet unable to stay in one place for more than a few minutes.

Noon came and went. He didn't bother with the midday meal. He walked and sat, and walked again. The longest day of his whole life moved infinitesimally along its chosen path.

How many times he walked past the white bulk of Kramer's building he didn't know. He was drawn there by the magnet of information which did not come. The sun grew hazed above him as storm clouds built up from the east, but he didn't notice the increasing humidity or the growing quietude which foreran the gathering storm.

It was late afternoon, and growing blacker, when the lean figure of Simon came out of the main door and ran down the wide drive, shouting to attract his attention.

"Benbow, hey, Benbow."

He stopped as Simon came up to him, and already the heavy, black drops of thundery rain were splashing on the white, dry concrete.

"Kramer wants you."

"Is there any news?"

"The plane is on its way—well on its way. It's due to land in half an hour."

Benbow stared at him wild eyed. "Why didn't you call me sooner?"

"Would it have helped?" The rain was heavier, splashing

138

in pattering drops more and more heavily. "Let's get inside. There is a storm building up. Salinger's plane is coming right through the heart of it. They've had a rough trip."

They ran for the main entrance, and Benbow asked, "What —what news is there?"

"None." Simon shook his head and refused to meet Benbow's agonized gaze. "Salinger hasn't given any indication."

"In heaven's name, why not?"

"I don't know."

A scout car came from the back of the building, rain splashing from the shining body. It pulled up before the main entrance just as they reached shelter, and almost at the same moment the bent form of Kramer, leaning heavily on a stick to aid his false leg, came out and joined them.

He waved the stick to Simon and Benbow. "Get in. Benbow, your moment of truth is close upon you."

"And yours upon you, Kramer," snapped Benbow grimly. He wondered what Kramer would do, how he would react when he learned of the two great ships building on Diemos. Whatever happened Kramer had to be told, Benbow had decided that already. This was knowledge that he could not conceal whatever the result of Salinger's journey; this was knowledge that concerned all Mankind—not just him, or Kramer, or Drusilla.

He had used that knowledge for his own ends, and the final justification for his act was near at hand. Even now, with uncertainty and excitement bubbling within him, he wondered if the justification was strong enough.

Why had Salinger given no news on the radio? A word would have been enough. Yes—or no!

The rain lashed across the car and the screen wipers slashed patterns in the curtain of water. Anxiety gnawed at him, an inborn certainty that something was wrong, and not as his dreams foretold.

The car turned in through the entrance of the field and stopped outside the entrance to the main control block. The few yards from car to door saw them all saturated by the steady downpour that was made more insidious by the thunder that rumbled in the distance.

Inside the lobby an official greeted them with a salute

and said, "The plane is due to land in ten minutes, General."

Kramer nodded absently and shook the water from his cap. They followed the official into a small, bare reception room to one side of the lobby. The tin leg creaked as Kramer took possession of the only chair. Simon leaned against the wall, his lips pursed and his forehead creased by a worried frown.

For Benbow there was only the jerky pacing of nervous tension. Why hadn't Salinger said anything? Anxiety mounted until there an edge of panic to his anticipation. His mind created questions that had to be answered, but ten minutes was too long for any man to wait under such strain. He wiped the sweat from his brow and noticed that his hand trembled as he did so.

Outside, the rain was a steady, roaring downpour that lashed upon the small window of the lobby room.

"Relax, Benbow," rasped Kramer.

"Damn you, Kramer. Can't you understand?"

"All too well." The single eye did not possess its usual brilliance. "You fear and you hope at one and the same time. But all your fear and all your hope won't change the ending that is already written. Relax."

"Go to the devil."

The door opened and the same official entered.

"She's on final approach, General. Touchdown in three minutes."

"Can we go out?" asked Benbow.

"In this weather?" Kramer snorted. "They'll be some minutes taxi-ing back."

"Anything is better than this damned room." Benbow went out of the office and stood just inside the main entrance. The air was stifling; the rain seemed to have the lobby penned in by its ferocity. Benbow was sweating profusely as much from nervous tension as from the effects of the humidity.

He could hear, far off and over the steady roaring of the storm, a hum like a bee swooping on a flower, growing by the second. Eagerly he looked for it, but the rain reduced visibility to little more than a few hundred feet, and his eyes ached with the effort of staring. There were footsteps behind him and he turned to find Kramer and Simon behind him.

"You, too?" he said, and resumed his searching.

The hum was a roar that competed with the storm in intensity; it filled the sky and the wide area of the landing field. And then the plane was upon them, coming in from the east, dropping like a great silver bird through the swirling blanket of rain on to the shining ribbon of the runway. It touched down less that a quarter of a mile away and vanished into the distance, blanketed by the rain. The high whine of the engines died.

"Can we go out in the car?" demanded Benbow.

"Take it easy," said Simon. "It'll start back in a moment."

A gray shape loomed out of the rain, and they could see the plane turning broadside on. The silhouette foreshortened and grew larger, a hum sounded over the roar of the storm. Benbow stood like a statue and watched it draw near, a great, gleaming bird that turned sideways a few short yards away from the control tower. The engines died and left the field to possession by rain and storm and distant thunder.

In the body of the plane a black oval appeared as the main hatch opened, and from within the black orifice the thin steps of the gangway moved smoothly down to the ground below.

Benbow walked forward hesitantly, out of the doorway and into the teeming rain, and his steps were as uncertain as he felt. He focused his whole attention on the black doorway, unaware of the rain that saturated him in seconds, that plastered his hair across his forehead and ran in rivers down his cheeks. Every fiber of his being was bent to the task of trying to see what was happening beyond—inside the plane. His footsteps quickened and he was unaware of Kramer and Simon following into the storm and across the wet tarmac. He stopped at the foot of the gangway and as he looked up the plump form of Salinger appeared in the hatch. The fat man stood for a moment and looked down at him; then he came slowly down the steps.

Benbow's tongue was a dry in his mouth, and his throat was clogged by uncontrollable emotion.

141

"Salinger," he called above the roaring rain, "why didn't you let me know?"

The dark eyes were sad, the bags under them were darker and heavier; they were the eyes of a man who had gone for many hours without sleep; a man who has thought and worried, but who has nothing to show for the labors of his conscience.

"Why, Salinger?"

"Because I daren't." Rain ran in rivulets from his peaked cap and his dark eyes were fixed almost hypnotically on Benbow. "This, Benbow, you have to learn for yourself. It can't be done by remote control."

Benbow felt his stomach weaken within him, panic seized his limbs, and in the open hatch another figure stood outlined, looking down at him. The figure of a woman in a shabby, gray mackintosh that was too large for her; the figure of a woman with a child cradled in her arms, shielded under the coat from the drenching downpour.

Benbow blinked the rain from his eyes and raised a hand to shield them, his emotions in turmoil as the rain prevented quick recognition. The woman came slowly down the gangway, and he could see that it was Drusilla. She was thinner than he remembered, even under the bulk of the coat he could see that, her hair was untidy with a streak of gray across the front. But it was Drusilla. And she had a child in her arms.

"Drusilla?"

He felt emotion die within him. There were questions being born in the chaos of his mind, for the child could not have been more than a few months old. Beyond her a man stepped from the body of the plane and hurried down the gangway to stand just behind her. Even through his bewilderment Benbow could recognise Hillary under a heavy beard—Hillary who led by the hand a small boy who struggled to press close to him, seeking protection from the rain. The boy must have been well over two years old.

Drusilla had come to him.

XXIV

BENBOW DIDN'T remember how he got back to the control tower. He couldn't recall, ever afterwards, the dazed bewilderment with which he viewed a situation so catastrophic as to be quite beyond his comprehension. It was the complete and utter antithesis of all his thoughts and dreams for so many months, and, as such, it carried within it the seeds of a disbelief so great that his mind told him he was living a nightmare from which he would awaken at any moment.

The awakening never came.

Drusilla's face swam before him, gaunt and ravaged, with haunted eyes that shed tears down the lines of her face—tears that mingled with the raindrops.

"I couldn't wait, Peter. God forgive me, I couldn't wait."

Dimly, he heard Simon cursing luridly. "Why didn't you leave them there, Joe? Christ, what a mess! Why did you bring them back? What good does it do?"

"Would he have believed me?" asked Salinger, and his voice reflected his physical weariness. "And, anyway, they had to come. There was nothing left for them at Butere. The other man, O'Brien, died of fever two months ago, and they've been living on a knife edge ever since."

"Even so—" Simon turned away.

The news of O'Brien's death did no more than rest on the surface of Benbow's mind. He was beyond shock, though regret would come later.

"It seems that O'Brien was the only man who could hold the area together," said Salinger. "The native chiefs respected him and helped him to retain a measure of civilized control. Once he'd gone the whole thing fell apart."

Benbow sat slumped on the chair, his whole body slack, his eyes seeing things that didn't really register on his stunned brain. Beyond the door, in the lobby, Kramer's voice boomed and echoed, the words were quite unintelligible.

"I'm sorry, Benbow." Salinger's voice was gentle, but it tugged at his attention. "Benbow, you understand, don't you? I couldn't do anything else. I had to bring them back."

"Why didn't you warn me?" Benbow's voice rasped from an arid throat.

"I thought about it. I decided this was something you had to face yourself—finally—once and for all. You can't do it secondhand." He paused. "I remembered when my wife was killed. . . ."

Benbow put his face in his hands. After all this time! The years of thought and hope, of anticipation, of planning and dreaming and wondering. And now. . . !

"Peter!"

He looked up. Drusilla stood before him, tall and gaunt and brown, her hair was wet and bedraggled, the gray coat wet with rain. She was a haggard copy of the girl he had carried for so long in his mind's eye. The dregs of beauty still clung to her, but it was shadowed by worry and hardship, by lack of food and proper nourishment. He realized with a pang that the years had dealt hard with her.

"Peter, you were on Mars. I thought that I would never see you again." The words, slow and careful to begin, came tumbling from her lips in a torrent of agitation. "He was there and you were not. He looked after the child, guarded us both. . . . Peter!" She stopped, her lips writhing desperately to find expression that would not come.

"The child?"

"I called him Peter. He thinks—" She broke off abruptly and looked away.

"That Hillary is his father?"

She said nothing. There was nothing left to say.

The shock was fading now, and Benbow felt only tired, resigned and empty. There was regret that his efforts over the past three years had been wasted on so unworthy a cause. The revulsion of shock was hard upon him. Perhaps if there had been someone on Mars? But there wasn't. . . . there never had been. There had been no one but Drusilla, not then, not now—not ever.

It is better to travel than to arrive.

Benbow laughed hysterically as the thought came to him, and he didn't notice the quick glance that passed between Simon and Salinger. The hysteria was quickly killed. Benbow thought about Mueller and Svenson, and about the two ships on Diemos. Would it be better for them to travel than to arrive?

"Will you take us back to Mars with you, Peter?"

Her question hit him like a physical blow, and his eyes opened wide with astonishment. Take them back to Mars! And this time the laughter was genuine and incredulous.

"I'm not going back to Mars, Dru. There's nothing there for me or for you or for anyone. Haven't you heard? Didn't Salinger enlighten your journey here? Earth is on the mend, and Man is on the way back." He smiled sadly. "I came back to find you and the child, to live with you and watch over you, to die with you if necessary. But it wasn't necessary. It never was necessary—only I was too stupid to realize it."

And as he spoke he knew what it was about her that now repelled him. She was pleading for salvation and forgiveness, but she was still too proud to ask outright. The result was an unpleasant mixture of pride and prevarication. If only she had said, "I am sorry for you, Peter, but not for what I have done," then he would have understood. But the years had changed her and hardship had taken something from her. Now, she wheedled and whined, her hands kneading together as she stood there, and there was not the defiance or the independence for which he had loved her. He knew it suddenly and starkly, and the results of his introspection were painful and unpleasant.

"Where is Kramer?" he asked Salinger, striving to break the circle in which he was trapped.

"Outside."

"It's time that we talked together." He stood up and managed a crooked smile at Drusilla. "Don't worry, Dru. Everything will be all right. I have much to thank Hillary for, without him—" he hesitated. "Well, no matter."

He followed Salinger to the door and went out into the lobby. The rain still poured from a lowering sky, and Kramer paced the floor, hunch shouldered, his tin leg bobbing ludicrously. Two or three other men stood around, and all of them turned as Benbow entered the lobby.

Kramer fixed him with his one good eye, and Benbow could see the lines of worry and concern etched deep in the old man's lean, pale face.

"Well, is it over?"

Benbow nodded. "Yes, Kramer, it's over. I suppose Salinger was right, though I would have argued the point with him a few hours ago."

"And what of our bargain?"

"I would have stood by it whatever the result." He smiled wryly. "Though no result could have been as bad as this."

"Then let us talk," snapped Kramer, and the old fire was back within him. "We'll talk out in the car. There, we'll not be disturbed." He raised his voice. "Joe, get Simon out here."

They walked out into the rain, but all of them were so wet that the few yards to the car made little appreciable difference. Kramer climbed into the driver's seat and Benbow slid in beside him. Simon and Salinger got in the back.

The rain hammered on the roof and pounded off the bonnet.

"Well, get on with it."

Benbow cleared his throat and wondered where he should begin. He thought of Mars and the ramshackle collection of huts that nestled under the tenuous domes of plastic. He thought of the red sand, and the cold nights, and the thin air; he thought of the poor plants, the sand storms, the lack of water—and he knew where he had to start.

"To tell you this, Kramer," he said slowly, "to help you understand, I must tell you what it's like on Mars. You think it is a good place to be because of the strong base that we have there. You think it is good because of the reports that Mueller has sent back telling of the progress that has been made." He paused and licked his lips. "To put it into clear perspective, just suppose for an instant that those reports were made with one end in view—to convince you, and all the people here at White Sands, that what they are doing was justified, that their efforts were bearing fruit. Just suppose that your strength here at White Sands was bolstered and maintained by the news you had from Mars." He looked at Kramer. "Mueller and his aides knew that if they told you the truth then White Sands would wither and die."

He could read nothing in the chalk white face.

"Think of a shanty town, Kramer, a poor, wretched ghost town huddled in the middle of a desert. I remember seeing one as a child in an old western film. I expect you have. Take that town and put it under a thin, fragile dome. Fill the dome with dessicated, sterile air. Build rough, hardboard huts, and cram them with people. Take men who have lost their families, women who have lost their husbands, people who are struggling to create something out of nothing. Think of them living on a knife edge, relying on Earth for everything, the food they eat, the clothes they wear, the tools they use. Picture them at the wrong end of a thin, tenuous line of ships stretching over millions of miles back to their home world—a line that may snap any moment and maroon them on a hostile world."

"But this is wrong," breathed Simon.

"Is it?" snapped Benbow. He looked at the shocked face of Simon and felt a twinge of pity. He knew that he was destroying a vision for all of them. Well, it had to be done.

He went on talking, telling them about the red sand and the storms, the poor vegetation, the water that had to be rationed, the food that was slop. He painted a picture of utter and complete desolation where nerves were stretched like bow strings. He told them of Martha Dresden and her dead child, and how she had died for no other reason than that she didn't want to live. He spoke of Mueller, rarely leaving his small office; of Larson and of Svenson and all the others who worked until it was time to sleep, and who rose to work again. Within his mind, as he talked, he drew pictures which were conjured into words, and as the canvas was filled he could see the disbelief growing within them, a disbelief that changed slowly to horror and bewilderment—and finally to fear.

And at last the picture was completed. There remained only the final coat of varnish.

"There you have it, Kramer. This is the empire you dreamed about, the stepping stone to the conquest of space. Do you still want it? Is it that important to you?"

"There is more, Benbow," Kramer whispered. "I know there is more." The one eye was bleak and cold. "You have set your scene well, but that is all you've done. Now, the rest of it."

147

Benbow nodded. "All right. Knowing all this that I have told you, living with it as Mueller has done for all these years, what would you have done, Kramer? Or you, Simon, Salinger?"

"Mueller is a scientist. He thinks with a brain that I do not possess," replied Kramer.

"Mars cannot be tamed," put in Salinger. "Man cannot live there for more than a few years. Is that what you're telling us?"

Benbow nodded.

"Therefore," said Salinger, "Man must leave Mars."

Kramer stared at Benbow. "You mean they are coming home? That you are the first?"

"No, that's too easy an answer." Benbow looked away across the rainswept area of the field. "They are building two great ships, Kramer, two small worlds with everything that is necessary for them to live for years—for generations if need be. They are sending them out into deep space, to other stars, seeking other worlds where they can build and live and flourish. Those ships are on Diemos, and they are almost completed."

XXV

IT WAS TOO big for them to take in all at once. He could see it in their faces and read it in their reactions. They were thinking about something that was entirely new, and he realized how very hard it must be for them. After all, he had seen it at firsthand; he had learned the hard way; for them, there was only the word picture that he had painted, a concept rather than a fact.

And Kramer reacted to the concept.

"We must stop them," he whispered, half to himself. "They mustn't be allowed to get away with it."

"If you had told them that the Weed was dying," Benbow told him, "and the process was being reversed, do you think that they would have gone on with it? The experts would have flocked home to salvage what they could and to prepare for the rebuilding of Earth. They'll still come, Kramer, if you tell them now. No man wants to cast himself adrift in the Universe if he can come home. No man will imprison himself in a steel coffin if he can breathe the airs of Earth—yes, even with the sulphur and the Weed to poison it for a few more years."

Kramer was hardly listening. The words eddied around him but they made no impression. He was still a prisoner of his own mind as he said, "Joe, we must get a force away as soon as possible. How soon can it be done?"

Benbow laughed incredulously. "You just don't understand, do you, Kramer?"

"I understand treason," rasped the General. "And I know how to deal with it."

"Treason that you have bred. What will you do when you get there? Hang Mueller? Shoot him? And what about the others that stay with him? What about me?"

"Damn you and damn Mueller." Kramer's mouth was a tight, thin line, the lips white and compressed. "I should have known that something like this was in the wind. When you came back—" He stopped speaking, his face deathly pale, the one eye a blaze of fury and frustration. "How long, Joe?"

Salinger looked at Benbow, and his face was bloodhound sad as he said, "I don't think it matters how long, General."

"It doesn't," agreed Benbow. "It'll take you weeks to prepare. Months before you can get your force to a point where it can exert any pressure. By that time the ships will be gone and there'll only be Mueller and few hundred others left. The experts that you need here, on Earth, will be gone forever."

"He's right," said Simon. "If, as he says, the ships are almost ready—"

"We don't know that—not for sure." But there was doubt in Kramer's voice as he spoke. The fury was dying and an air of indecision was taking its place.

"You don't know about any of it—not for sure," taunted Benbow. "You have only my word for it. You daren't take the risk of ignoring what I have said because it just might be true. And you have only one way out."

"What is that?" asked Salinger.

"Tell Mueller what has happened here on Earth. I'll back

149

you up and I shall be believed. Tell him that you need every man that can be sent. He'll co-operate." He grinned suddenly. "In ten years, Kramer, the whole North American continent can be under full control again."

"It won't be easy," Simon said. "There'll be the quakes and the volcanoes—"

"Nothing is ever easy," countered Benbow. "Not getting to Mars or building the base or sending the people and the supplies. Do you think it was easy to build those two ships on Diemos? The men who did that will make mincemeat of a job like rebuilding their home world."

Kramer got stiffly out of the car and walked away from them across the sodden tarmac. It had stopped raining but none of them had noticed it until now. The clouds were still heavy and gray, the air moist and humid. Benbow moved to follow Kramer, but Simon put out a hand and stopped him. Kramer paused and stood some yards away, his hands clasped behind his back and his head bowed in thought.

"He isn't as bad as you may think, Benbow," said Simon. "He needs time to think about things. He isn't a young man, and all his adult years have been spent in fighting the Weed, in fighting anarchy and revolt. He sees force as an end in itself because he has lived by force for too long. Give him time—he isn't a fool."

Time, thought Benbow. God how much time do we have? How much time had been wasted already? If he hadn't come back to Earth . . . If he hadn't acted like a lovesick schoolboy, chasing something that had been dead for a long, long time . . .

"Those ships will be ready in five months or less, Simon," he said coldly. "Mueller was aiming to get them away within a year at the time I left Mars. If I know him and his men, then his timing won't be very far out."

Kramer turned slowly and commenced his peglegged return. He walked slowly, an old man with the weight of a world upon his shoulders. Benbow felt a twinge of pity; in years gone by, the General would have retired by now. He would have been sitting in a sunlit garden, dreaming of a life that was past. Yet here, at White Sands, he worked and slogged as hard as any man, and he bore upon his

150

crippled body a burden greater than any man had known before in the history of the World.

He stopped beside the car and looked at Benbow through the open door. "We have no choice, have we, Benbow? Mueller must be told—his plans must be altered. The process of supply can be reversed. The men and women must be brought back here."

"They can start arriving in five or six months," said Salinger.

"If the ships are nearly ready on Diemos, surely they could be used?" put in Simon.

"Yes," Kramer nodded. "Yes. That way we could get every single person back here within the year." He swung himself into the driving seat, and switched on the engine. "We'll get working on it at once, gentlemen."

He moved the car off towards the entrance to the field, and Simon said, "What about the driver, General?"

Kramer laughed out loud, the first time Benbow had seen humor in him. "The walk will do him good." They drove through the gates and he said, "Joe, when can we raise Mars on a direct contact?"

"I'll have to check," replied Salinger, "but I think it may be some time during the early evening."

They got back to Kramer's headquarters, and already Benbow could see a change in the man. He had cast off his outworn ideas of conquest like a snake sloughing off its unwanted skin. He reacted now as a man should who has decision and responsibility at his command. There was a complete change in his manner, and Benbow knew that the fresh concept was making itself felt. Simon and Salinger were more optimistic, and long before they reached Kramer's office they were eagerly making plans.

Once inside, Salinger reached for a large file and consulted it for several seconds. He did a few rapid calculations on a sheet of paper, and then announced. "We can raise Mars base between seven forty-seven and nine twenty-three tonight, General."

Kramer nodded. "Well, that gives us time to prepare our message."

The clock on the wall told Benbow that it was a little after four, and he realized that he hadn't eaten since that morning. The midday meal had passed in an agony of anticipation, and now he was weak and empty, drained of emotion, at once hungry for food and sick at the thought of it.

"There's nothing I can do here," he said. "I'll freshen up and get some food."

"You'll be back." Kramer made the statement.

"Yes, of course."

"Will you be all right?" asked Salinger.

Benbow smiled his gratitude. "Yes, I'll be all right. It's over now."

He left the office and walked back to his quarters. He felt tired and stale; his clothes were wet upon his body, and his head ached. He felt as if he hadn't slept for a long, long time. He knew that sleep would be hard to come by tonight.

He thought about Drusilla and Hillary and the child—the children, and he realized that now he could think about it objectively. There was regret, but there was no pain. He should never have left Earth in the first place, but it was past the time for thoughts like that. He had no more idea what her life must have been like on Earth than she had of his on Mars. Each had been an existence quite beyond the comprehension of the other. Hillary had been there to help her. He had not. Hillary was a strong, kindly and competent man—Benbow knew that from his own experience. He had been around, and Benbow had not. It was as simple as that.

He washed himself in brown, tepid water in the quiet of his small room; he put on clean clothes, combed his hair and went down to the mess hall to eat. It was nearly half past five, and he had almost two hours to kill.

There were few people there when he entered, but those few included Drusilla and Hillary. He couldn't avoid them.

He collected his food from the counter and took it across to their table.

He sat down, and asked, "How are you, Hillary?"

"Well enough. And you?" The eyes above the fierce, black beard were surprising calm and gentle.

Benbow smiled. "I am well—now." He looked at the boy

152

who sat between his parents and fumbled awkwardly with a large spoon. "He looks remarkably healthy."

"We did our best. It wasn't easy."

"No, I suppose not." Suddenly, Benbow wasn't hungry. There was a hard knot in his stomach, as he realized that the boy would never be his. Drusilla was committed, Hillary was committed and—worst of all—the child was committed. There was nothing that Benbow could do about it. Indeed there was nothing that he wished to do about it.

He stood up abruptly, leaving the food untouched on the bare, wooden table.

"Go on doing your best, Hillary," he said, "for all of them."

He walked out of the mess hall without looking back.

XXVI

THE EVENING was dark and humid as he walked from his room back to Kramer's headquarters. Thunder rumbled in the distance and the clouds were thick and black in the evening sky. The taint of sulphur seemed stronger, and he guessed that storm winds had brought it in from the quake-ridden Pacific. He was thankful that it had replaced the stench of the Weed.

Fresh quakes and volcanoes were being registered almost daily on the instruments of the base as the Earth shook and convulsed. Benbow knew—as did everyone else—that these convulsions would continue for a long time, but the thought held no terror now. There had been terror in the days when the Weed was strong, when the mists swirled and billowed, covering the sea and the land with their all-pervading presence.

Now, the seas were shaking off the shackles of the Weed; the wind and the weather were coming into their own again. There would be storms such as the world had not seen for millions of years, but the very fact of rain and wind and storm meant that the poisonous sulphur fumes would be washed and filtered from the atmosphere. The death of the Weed meant the dispersal of the mists which would hold the sulphur and concentrate its stinking, yellow micro-drops. The rain would counter the effects of the mists, and the danger to human and animal life would be removed.

When summer ended, the storms that would hit White Sands would make the one he had seen this day look small and feeble. They would bring about the suspension of rocket flights; planes would be grounded; the work of rebuilding would be held up. With it all, though, they would be necessary evils.

Benbow felt happier than he had been for a long time. The weight of worry and anticipation was lifted from him, and he knew that the worst was behind him. The desperation of the past years was a thing to be forgotten; there would be hard work ahead of him, but that was nothing new; it would be the work of rebuilding and the end would be worth all the effort because it would be the end that all men wanted. There would be no steel coffin with two thousand souls living and dying across the deeps of space; there would be no grand evacuation from a world that was slowly ceasing to exist; there would be something other than a future that was bleaker than the past which had gone before. Whatever happened during the next months and years would be better than what had preceded it.

Salinger met him in the brightly lit entrance hall, and he greeted Benbow with a smile. "Ready for the big night?"

Benbow returned his smile; Salinger's obvious excitement was infectious, and he felt a tide rising within him that was something wonderful—something he had not known for many years. It was an emotion that he had thought was dead, yet now, with hope reborn, he knew that Mankind's innate resilience was being rekindled.

Together they went along the corridor to Kramer's office. Inside was pandemonium with twenty or more men and women gathered in groups, talking with an animation that was exhilarating to hear. Benbow's tiredness was a long way behind him.

"Benbow," Kramer bellowed at him from behind his desk. "I thought you were going to miss the fun. We're just leaving for the radio room."

The change in Kramer was astonishing. He seemed to stand straighter as he rose from his chair, and there was a hint of a smile around the tight mouth that went a long way toward dissipating the grim set of his craggy face. The eye, which was normally so forbidding and so cold, held a sparkle of anticipation that seemed almost out of place.

Kramer limped across to the door, and Salinger nodded to Benbow to follow him. Simon was there, and there were others, men and women whom Benbow knew by sight, people who nodded and smiled at him with a recognition that was pleasing. He was the one who had brought them the news.

The radio building lay away from the main block, a low one-storied building with four giant masts that reached up into the dark night. The windows were brightly lit and they seemed almost garish under the storm clouds. Inside the main control room there were more people waiting for them. The console was a gray monolith against one wall, its panels and dials and switches gleaming in the brilliant electric light. Greens and reds and yellows shimmered and flickered on the face of it, and men and women in shirt sleeves sat in padded chairs with the hum and whine of equipment providing a background to the low, murmurous chatter that rose and fell like a tide.

Kramer went straight over to the console and one of the operators nodded to him as he approached. "All set, General. We should have contact in about three minutes."

"Is this manually controlled?" Benbow asked.

Salinger shook his head. "No, the tolerances are too tight. There's an automatic beam-locking device that cuts in as soon as we're in contact. We have a teleprinter linked to the main receiver, and messages come out on that screen in front of the chief controller."

"How long before we get a reply?"

Salinger shrugged. "Half an hour at least."

"By that time this room will be like a furnace."

"Everyone wants to be in on it," grinned Salinger. "You can't blame them. For once we seem to be heading in the right direction—and everyone knows it."

Benbow stood and looked at the people around him. They talked and gestured and sweated under the harsh lights; there was an animation about them that raised a tension inside him and Benbow knew that he couldn't stay here and watch them as they waited.

"I'm going outside, Salinger," he said abruptly. "Call me when you hear."

He pushed towards the door anxious to escape the claustrophobic effect of the crowded room. When he got outside the humidity seemed cool by comparison. He walked across the wide area of sodden lawn and he felt the tension lift from him a little. He wondered what time it was on Mars, what Mueller would be doing, and Svenson; he thought about Larson and his interminable spirituals, about Chen Su and his motherless children. If only Martha could have held on a little longer.

There would be so much to do now, an ever increasing effort that would have to be mounted against heavy odds. Benbow knew that those odds would not be as heavy as they had been before, and it was this which dictated his mood and the mood of all the others gathered in that hot, stuffy room, waiting. It was this knowledge that brightened their lives, for they knew now what it was they were fighting —what it was they were up against.

Mankind had conquered Earth before, and Earth would be conquered again, given the knowledge and the help of the people on Mars, the experts who had been sent to safety so that the race could survive. Now, the race would survive, and there was joy in the knowledge.

He heard his name being called, and he turned to see the plump form of Salinger outlined in the doorway.

"Benbow, we're in contact. The message is going out."

"I'll come in presently," he replied.

The light vanished, but Salinger hadn't gone back inside. He crossed towards Benbow, a dark figure backed by the light from a window.

"Why the hermit act, Benbow?"

"I don't know." He hesitated. "Perhaps, after all this time, I need to be alone. You know, Salinger, I can remember England before the Weed. I can remember days at school when the world was bright and sunny, when the sea was cool and blue and soft. It seems so long ago that it's like a dream. To me, this is the real world—the Weed and the mists and the quakes and the volcanoes. Japan lost forever, New York destroyed—a myth that'll never be reborn. This is the reality that I've lived with for too long to believe that it will end soon."

"Yes, I know."

They stood in silence for a long minute, and then Salinger said, "I'm going back in. Don't be too long."

"Call me if anything happens."

"I will."

He left Benbow alone with his thoughts.

The minutes passed and the black clouds swept over his head. His hair and shoulders were wet with the gathering dampness of the night, and just as he had felt the claustrophobia of the hot room so he felt the agoraphobia of the darkness outside. The oppressiveness of the gathering night drove him back to the company of his fellow men.

Inside the radio room the atmosphere was stifling, but there was almost complete silence. Excitement lay heavily, an all embracing pall, as the waiting men and women stood around and shuffled their feet in small movements of impatience.

Salinger nodded to Benbow. "I was coming to fetch you. We should be getting a reply through any minute now."

Kramer nodded at him, and smiled tautly, but there was tension in the smile—the same sort of tension that flooded the room. There was anticipation and eagerness, an excitement that bubbled and effervesced but which did not transmit itself to Benbow as he leaned against the wall beside the door and waited.

He felt a premonition that twisted his stomach, and the claustrophobic effect of that hot, crowded room was back with him again. He turned away and looked out the half open door into the blackness of the night.

Behind him a click sounded from the console, a small sound that echoed above the hum of the main generator. It seemed to galvanize the muscles of the waiting groups, and he could sense the sudden tensing of their bodies even though he could not see them.

"Contact," called the Controller.

Benbow went outside. He was breathing heavily as though he had been running for a long time, and there was a sickness inside him that was born of terror. The grass was soft under his feet, and it was raining again. In the distance thunder rumbled, an ominous noise that added to the oppression in which he stood.

He wiped the sweat from his brow and thought of Mueller with his wire spectacles perched on his button nose. They would be askew as always. He wondered what emotions would be engendered, and he thought of that time when the messages had spoken of Earth's end, of the volcanoes and the earthquakes. He remembered the silent crowds that had gathered outside Mueller's office, waiting, watching, weeping for that which they thought was lost to them forever.

If only Kramer had told the truth so much time and trouble and unhappiness would have been saved.

From inside the radio room came shouts and uproar. Benbow felt his whole body trembling as if he had a fever. The agony of premonition was tearing at him as he heard screams and shouts mounting on a tide of hysteria.

He could hear Salinger calling for him from within, and as he turned back towards the door, the bulky form came plunging out into the night. Salinger shouted, "Benbow! Benbow, where are you, damn you?"

"Here, Salinger—over here."

"Benbow, the ships!" The words were wrenched from him as Salinger shouted above the chaos in the background. "The ships have gone—they left Diemos eight weeks ago."

The trembling had stopped. Benbow stood quietly in an oasis of peace that nothing could disturb.

"They are beyond radio contact, Benbow. They've gone, damn you. We're too late."

"No, Salinger." He felt unutterably tired. "We're not too late now, we've just caught up, that's all. We were too late on the day Kramer decided not to tell Mueller that the Weed was dying. We were too late right from the beginning."

"What do we do? Benbow, for God's sake, what do we do?"

It was raining heavily now, and the thunder was so close that it shook the ground on which he stood. It wasn't the end, he thought, not quite; the chaos would pass and that would take a long time. The thing was that always in

158

the future they would have before them the picture of two giant steel coffins plunging deeper and deeper into the unknown, seeking for that which had never really been lost.

He shivered despite the humidity and turned back towards the brightness of the open door.